the
Art Collector

the Art Collector

KATELYN BREHM

To Tommi—

Thanks for reading!

Dedication

To Kel.
Your emotional support maracas made this novella
possible. Thank you for being you.

And to the city of Milwaukee.
I will forever consider you home.

Dresden, Germany, 1874

MY BODY WENT rigid as the sheet fell from the artist's barely-dry canvas and revealed the disturbing scene underneath.

A lovely, young woman lay in her bed, a picture of innocence draped in white linens, limbs flung overhead in the careless abandon of peaceful, deep sleep. Her creamy skin shone bright and flawless under a soft light, and a pale flush touched her cheeks, accentuating her plump pink lips.

Outside the serene glow surrounding the woman's lithe body, an ominous darkness permeated the painting. From the drapes hanging between the bedposts to the papered walls of the shadowy room, midnight blues and charcoal grays swirled in a mélange to disguise the faint outline of a sinister figure looming over her sleeping form.

The use of dark tones and wide brushstrokes created a ghostlike presence, a mere suggestion of a monstrous being, which only served to emphasize what the artist did make visible—the devilish features of a demonic face. The creature looked down its hawkish nose at the innocent woman, an avaricious sneer across thin lips as it reached out with boney, long-nailed fingers to her exposed breast.

Its eyes, the most haunting feature of the monster's lurid face, glowed an iridescent green and shone through the darkness of the shadowed background like lanterns illuminated from within.

At least he got the eyes right, I thought, my cynicism tempering my bitterness.

"Is it final?" I asked through clenched teeth as I turned to face the artist.

He stared at me in that eccentric way artists did, eyes intense and boring straight through to my soul. His disheveled countenance suggested he hadn't slept much the night before. Not surprising given the deadline, the subject, or the customer.

"Yes, sir," he replied, breathless. "Finished last night. I tried to capture the creature's essence. The moment it preys on its victim. The baroness provided such a vivid description." He cleared his throat. "She has... quite the imagination."

"Quite."

"I hope my rendering does the baroness's vision justice."

"She will be pleased." Disdain filled my voice despite my best efforts to suppress it. I had no doubt the artist captured the impression the sick woman sought to elicit. "Have it wrapped. My footman will bring it out to my carriage." I held out a small purse, eager to be done with the loathsome task. "Your commission."

"Thank you, sir. And please, thank the baroness for her continued patronage."

"I'll be sure to pass along the message," I said dryly as I walked out of the gallery, no intention of speaking to the witch any more than necessary.

Art, in all its forms, manifested interpretation, an impression of the subject left on the artist, and these days, patrons paid heaping sums to ensure the artists' impressions matched their own. I paused. The baroness was not the only one in the family with money.

The bell rang when the door swung open, and my footman exited with the oversized oil. While he loaded the package into my carriage, I summoned the artist with a wave of my hand.

"A moment, please. Are you available for another commission? I would like a painting of my own."

Milwaukee, Wisconsin, 2022

I SHOOK MY head and huffed out a chuckle, the puff of warm air visible as it left my lips. My troublemaking teenage self would never have believed twenty-five years later she'd be driving to the Witch's House for work.

I exited the freeway and headed north on Lincoln Memorial Drive. The downtown Milwaukee skyline loomed outside my driver-side window while to my right the Calatrava unfurled its wings against the glistening backdrop of Lake Michigan.

The Witch's House. I snorted. A trip to the mysterious mansion had been a right-of-passage as a teen. Half-drunk on whiskey pilfered from our parents' liquor cabinets, masquerading in repurposed Snapple bottles, someone would suggest driving to the Witch's House after the coffee shops closed and we no longer had a place to chain smoke cigarettes while drinking over-sweetened and over-creamed coffee and declaring our self-important opinions on politics and world events.

Despite my thick cable-knit sweater, I shivered. I wrinkled my nose to get the blood flowing in my face again and twisted the loose ring on my finger, my hands shrunk from the cold. Early November's damp chill seeped into a person's bones, as if autumn could prepare anyone for what came next. I reached out and turned up the heat, wishing I had one of those fancy cars with seat warmers instead of my fifteen-year-old Jetta that still had knobs. But my trusty Volkswagen had survived this many winters; it could survive at least one more.

I cruised past the marina toward Lake Drive and the wealthy northern suburbs of the city. At six o'clock, rush hour traffic had started to subside. The sun hung low, obfuscated by the tall condo buildings lining the lakefront, its orange glow picturesque amid the brilliant fall colors that adorned the trees.

A stickler for completing my workday at five, my fascination with the Witch's House overrode my rigidity, making this after-hours excursion worth the overtime and the drive.

The couple of times I'd gone as a teen, we'd piled into someone's parent's car—or, if lucky, one of the rich kids' SUVs—and drove north along the lake through winding, tree-lined paths until we found the fabled mansion perched high on a bluff overlooking the lake. We parked and dared each other to hop the stone wall surrounding the property, testing each other's bravery—and sobriety—to inspect the bizarre, misshapen statues that dotted the front lawn. Our teenage minds went wild with theories, fueled by decades of local myth and marijuana.

Had the woman who lived there killed her husband and child, and thrown them over the bluff into the icy waters of the lake? Were the statues the remains of teenagers, like us, frozen in place for trespassing? Or was she a serial murderer, marking the graves of her victims with sculpted tombstones?

I huffed out another breathy laugh and shook my head at the ridiculous rumors and memories from high school. More likely than not, the "witch" who'd lived there was a shut-in or a recluse, and a mundane explanation existed for the bizarre sculptures. I couldn't resist the temptation to discover the truth when my boss asked me to take the job. My curiosity piqued those many years ago, the mystery of the mansion now called to me like a siren.

I worked for a high-end consignment firm—Parker & Sons Real Estate and Consignment—specializing in estate sales for owners whose property could be traced back generations. Most of the time, the individuals inheriting the old homes didn't care what we found inside, or for the property itself, eager to consign the contents and use the money to buy a flashy, high-rise condo with a killer view of the lake. As a specialist in art history and antiques, I catalogued and appraised the properties' contents, helping ensure the new owners got top dollar for the treasures left behind.

When my boss Mr. Parker told me the new owner of the Witch's House wanted an appraisal of the estate's artwork, I jumped at the chance regardless of the appointment time. I could only imagine the priceless and unique objet d'art I might find inside and refused to pass up an opportunity to unlock its mysteries.

And it's not like I had anything better to do on a Monday night. My social calendar wasn't exactly overflowing with options.

My cell phone buzzed in the cup holder. I glanced down and smiled at the caller. I hit the answer button and put my little sister on speaker.

"Hey."

"Hey," Christine said. "Whatcha doin'?"

"Driving."

"Wanna come over for dinner?"

"Can't."

"Oh?" she asked with an optimistic lilt to her voice. Her interest annoyed me; I knew she hoped I had a date.

"Yeah, I have to work."

I waited for the inevitable commentary on my vacuous love life.

"At night?"

Her skepticism wasn't misplaced; I never worked past five, and my life was nothing if not predictable.

"The client wanted to meet tonight to get the project started, and Mr. Parker is bending over backwards to accommodate him. It's a huge contract. Lots of art, lots of money. You know Mr. Parker."

Wait for it.

"I'm not even going to comment on the fact you shouldn't be able to come to my house for dinner tonight not because you're working, but because you have a hot date."

And there it is.

I rolled my eyes.

"Don't roll your eyes at me, Mad," Christine continued, and I chuckled. "You're forty-three years old and single. You need to get out more even if it means spending less time with us."

My sister doled out opinions like leaflets shoved under your windshield wiper.

"Whatever," I replied, shutting her down with my flip response, a tactic I'd perfected long ago.

She let out an overexaggerated sigh. "So, where are you headed?"

"Get this. Remember that mansion north of the city—the Witch's House?"

"No way!"

"Yes way. I'm on Lake Drive right now heading up there."

"I need all the details."

"Apparently, the new owner inherited the estate from his mother when she died ten years ago, but he hasn't done anything with it since."

"I can't wait to hear what you find. Be careful, though. That place creeps me out. What if those old rumors were true?"

She paused, and I could almost hear the gears of her imagination whirring.

"What if the new owner is as evil as the old witch and throws you off the bluff?!"

I laughed. My sister could be... extra. She worked as a reporter for the *Shepherd Express* and was always on the hunt for a juicy story.

"Doubtful. The guy probably just didn't want to deal with it. He lives in Germany."

"Hm. Well. Keep me posted. I can't wait to hear what it looks like inside."

"Will do."

"Laters."

"Bye."

Despite my skepticism, Christine's ridiculous speculation and my high school memories sparked my imagination. What if there *was* a story there? I laughed aloud at the outrageous thought. No. This job would be as ordinary as the rest of my life.

Maybe it was the urban legends. Or maybe it was my excitement at getting selected to perform such an important job for the firm. Or maybe my life really had become too predictable. Whatever the reason, I couldn't wait to get started.

TURNING OFF LAKE Drive, I drove into the wooded side streets between the main thoroughfare and the lake. Oranges, reds, and yellows canopied the winding roads and blocked the remaining twilight as I followed the twisting paths toward the entrance. A low stone wall surrounded the property, crumbling in places and in desperate need of repair.

I rounded the corner, and the entry to the driveway came into view. Two weathered, yet domineering guardian lions stared down at me from atop stone pillars, monitoring any visitors approaching the wrought iron gates that barred their passage. I slowed to a stop and waited beneath their watchful eyes until, with a scream of rusted iron, both sides of the gate crept inward. My heart rate ticked up at the sound. I inched my car through the gaping maw of gothic metal, and the gates whined closed behind me as I traveled up the long, straight driveway toward the mansion.

The flickering light of dirty gas lamps, only half of which worked, illuminated the sculptures scattered across the broad expanse of the front lawn like ancient tombstones, worn and chipped with age from the harsh Wisconsin winters. Seen through the lens of my life's work, they looked different now than they had as a teen. I recognized the stone sculptures for what they were—modern art—and could identify the Symbolist and Realist influences that shaped each piece. Even so, the selection itself gave me pause—misshapen beasts with snarling faces and humans twisted almost beyond recognition—each sculpture exuding a sense of torture or at the very least pain. Weeds grew in giant stalks, browned from autumn, and clawed at their bases. Ivy wrapped around the legs of one particularly disturbing statue, a man's warped face turned up to the sky in an agonized scream as if he were being dragged down into a grave.

Why would someone curate such a grim collection? And why had the new owner let the property slip into such disarray? An uneasiness settled over me despite knowing there must be a rational answer to these questions. I shook off the absurd apprehension and refocused my attention on the task at hand.

I turned into a drive that circled an empty stone fountain in front of the impressive entrance that served as the centerpiece of the mansion's façade. The stone edifice stood like a bastion of another time. The cream-colored brick that gave Milwaukee its "Cream City" nickname combined with the burnt-red roof tiles to lend the mansion an old-world feel. Ivy climbed the building's corners, reaching out with twisting fingers toward the bay windows on either side of the grand entrance. Carved grotesques capped both windows, and their thick drapes obscured the view inside. Small stone balconies outside the four sets of second-story windows brought further character to its face, and steep roofs with pointed peaks topped the tall third story. The mansion looked like an abandoned castle from another time.

I turned off the circle into the garage on the west side of the property and pulled alongside a silver Porsche with racing wheels. I winced at the thought of the rust patches on the driver-side rear bumper of my Jetta. I was so out of my element here.

I walked up the steps of the covered portico and searched for the doorbell beneath the faint glow of the gas lamps on either side of the iron-inlaid wooden doors. Instead, I found an old bell pull, which I tugged. A deep gong resounded over the quiet rustling of leaves and the break of waves against the rocky bluff. The wind coming off the lake chilled me to the bone as I waited.

A light went on, shining through the stained-glass panels on either side of the door. I straightened my spine, tossed my mop of hair behind my shoulders, and smoothed my sweater over my jeans. I glanced down at my beat-up loafers and grimaced.

I hadn't planned on seeing any clients today and had forgone heels for comfort.

The door creaked open, and an old man in a three-piece suit stood on the other side of the threshold. Of medium height and build, he looked like a balding Einstein, his thinning, white hair sticking out at angles, a stark contrast to his impeccable attire. He must have been older than my parents, his face gaunt with deep lines and pale blue eyes hollowed beneath a bushy, unkempt brow.

"Good evening, madam," he said with a heavy accent and bow of his head. "How may I help you?"

"Hello. My name is Madelyn Frye. I'm the art appraiser from Parker & Sons Real Estate and Consignment."

"Ach, ja. Please come in."

I stepped over the threshold and into a foyer preserved from a bygone era. The edges of a marble floor formed a perimeter around a burgundy Oriental rug that complemented velvety damask wallpaper atop rich mahogany wainscoting. White sheets covered whatever paintings hung on the foyer walls as well as the entry table and sideboard. A dust- and cobweb-covered crystal chandelier hung from the steepled ceiling and cast a low, ghostly glow over the room.

The soft, melancholic notes of classical piano drifted into the foyer. A Chopin prelude. The music called to me from the distance.

"I am Fritz, the von Dreiss family butler. Baron von Dreiss awaits you in the study."

"Oh," I fumbled, caught off guard by the title. "Nice to meet you, Fritz."

The music grew louder as the butler led me down a hallway to the left of the entrance toward the east end of the mansion and the lake. Dim lights flickered under dusty lampshades, and more sheet-covered artwork lined the walls. The musty smell of damp wood and old linens hung in the stale air. The hall ended at a doorway that opened into the eastern-most room of the first floor. The door stood half open, and the warm glow of light from within penetrated the darkness of the hallway as we approached.

The butler stopped before the door and held his arm out in a gesture indicating I should enter. I pushed the door open and stepped forward into the room, looking back at him for assurance. He nodded to me once, turned, and walked back toward the foyer.

To my right, a fireplace blazed, filling the room with light and warmth. An antique, Victorian desk faced away from the fireplace and into the room.

Tall French doors lined half the eastern wall partially covered by thick taupe drapes and hinted at a magnificent view of the lake beyond. The rest of the room's details escaped me, my attention drawn to the grand piano at the north end of the ornate study.

Opposite the fireplace, a man sat hunched over the ivories, the piano's shiny black veneer glinting in the firelight. His medium-length wavy black hair threaded through with hints of silver hung in front of his face, hiding his features, but his slender body swayed to the music, and long fingers danced across the keys as the prelude reached its crescendo.

I leaned against the inside of the door jamb, mesmerized by the emotion pouring out of the piano through the dolorous notes. I loved Chopin, this prelude one of my favorites, and the man at the piano executed it to perfection. As the piece came to its musical denouement, the player looked up, and my breath caught in my chest.

High cheekbones and a straight nose beneath smooth olive skin startled me in their severity. Laugh lines creased the corners of his eyes and bracketed full lips, imparting experience and wisdom amplified by the angle of his strong, square jaw.

His eyes captured mine, and I lost myself in their verdant depths. Like pools of sea-glass, they sparkled in the firelight as if they shone from within. I'd never seen eyes that color, and they held me in thrall.

A wave of dark hair fell across his forehead, and he blinked long eyelashes as he brushed it aside. "Pardon my indulgence. I haven't played this piano in years," he said with the slightest of German accents. The way he pronounced *haven't* with a soft *f*, combined with his rich baritone, made my knees weak. "I had it tuned this afternoon and couldn't resist."

When he stood and took a step toward me, my heart beat faster in my chest. At least a half foot taller than me, his expensive, tailored clothes hugged his powerfully built, lean frame. He'd rolled up the shirtsleeves of his crisp, white button-down revealing muscled forearms that twitched as he picked up a snifter off the sideboard containing the last swig of a drink and lifted it to his lips. He reminded me of one of those refined, intelligent-looking men who blessed the pages of a Ralph Lauren ad, and the way he stared at me with those clear, green eyes left me speechless.

My appearance thrust itself to the forefront of my mind. My bulky sweater hid the curve of my waist, doing me and my hourglass figure zero favors, and I couldn't remember if I'd put on makeup that morning.

Wait. Why the hell was I self-conscious? The man standing across from me was a client, not a date. I pulled myself together, determined to break the near palpable tension between us, and cleared my throat.

"Mr. von Dreiss. I'm Madelyn Frye from Parker & Sons Real Estate and Consignment. You asked for an appraiser to meet with you tonight to discuss your estate's artwork?"

My words came out quick and choppy, and the corner of his mouth turned up in a wry smirk as if he knew his presence unsettled me.

"A pleasure to meet you, Ms. Frye. Thank you for coming on such short notice. There is much to do to put this house to rights, and I am eager to get started."

He gestured to an upholstered chair on the opposite side of his desk, and I walked over and took a seat. He poured another splash of caramel-colored liquid into his snifter and glanced over his shoulder. "Would you care for a brandy?"

I smiled. Brandy. He'd feel right at home in Milwaukee.

"No. Thank you. I have to drive."

He capped the decanter, sauntered over to his desk, and sank into the high-backed Victorian desk chair crossing his legs. He set the snifter down on the

25

blotter and spun the glass with deft fingers. I looked up and met his eyes. He stared back at me, his steady gaze captivating. He appeared so proper and sophisticated yet exuded a primal sensuality that had butterflies taking flight in my stomach.

I blushed and cleared my throat. "The project?"

"The project," he replied. "As you may or may not know, this house has been empty for the past ten years since my mother died. I would like to restore the estate and make it my primary residence." He lifted the snifter and swirled the brandy under his nose, then took a sip. "The property suffered years of neglect, even before she died. The gardens and exterior are in complete disrepair, the fixtures and decor need an update, and the interior…" He looked around his study. "Well, my mother had eclectic taste."

"I see. And how do I fit in?"

"You, Ms. Frye, are going to catalogue and appraise the art hanging throughout the house. Help me decide what stays and what goes. My personal collection is in transit from the family estate in Germany, and I need help curating a selection."

"How much art are we talking about?" Considering the size of the mansion and the number of pieces in the study alone, the collection had to be vast.

"I don't have an exact number. My family has been collecting art for..." He seemed to consider his next words, and a smirk formed on his lips. "Generations." He took a sip of his drink. "Some of the pieces on these walls were hung when the mansion was first built in 1880. Others were purchased by my mother after my father and I moved to Germany in 1990. I had Fritz check the attic—it's empty. Every painting in this house is hanging on a wall. I suspect somewhere on the order of fifty, maybe sixty, pieces."

I swallowed. "That's a lot of art. This will be quite the undertaking."

"Quite. Which is why I wanted to get started right away, go over the project tonight before all manner of workers descend on my property. The gardeners arrive early tomorrow, the scaffolding for the exterior goes up mid-morning, and I will be in and out throughout the day. But you have already met Fritz. My housekeeper Mathilda flies in later tonight. They have been trusted family employees for years and will see to all your needs. They will open the rest of the rooms, remove the coverings, and clean. As they progress, you will be able to catalogue and appraise the art in each room."

Mr. Parker had presented me with a rare chance to view and appraise a private collection with significant potential—an opportunity most art historians only dreamed of—and I promised myself he wouldn't regret entrusting me with such an important project. "You made the right decision coming to Parker & Sons, Mr. von Dreiss. You won't be disappointed."

"Of that I have no doubt, Ms. Frye," he said with a mischievous grin.

Had I imagined the sensuality implicit in those words or the heat in his eyes? Regardless, his response to my innocent declaration caused an unexpected flutter in my chest.

"You may start your work in here tonight…" He gestured around the study with his brandy. "If you'd like."

I blinked. Surprised, but eager to make a good impression with an important client, I tried to sound nonchalant despite the rapid beat of my heart. "No time like the present," I said with a smile, and reached into my messenger bag for my leather-bound notebook and a pen.

"What, no tablet gadget or something?" he asked, amused.

"No. I suppose I'm old school like that. I prefer an actual paper and pen for notetaking in the field."

"Ah. A woman after my own heart." His eyes held mine as he lifted a hand to his heart and flashed a genuine smile that lit his face and made him impossibly more handsome.

My cheeks heated, and I looked away to survey the room before he saw me blush.

Artwork in antique frames from a variety of eras, schools, and artists decorated the walls. I let out a deep breath. Time to work.

A cluster of small paintings hung on the wall behind the piano in an artful arrangement indicative of someone with an eye for display composition. I stepped closer, taking notes on my overall impressions of the arrangement before cataloguing signatures, subjects, and mediums, not at all surprised by their age or the fact they were all originals. I recognized all but two of the signatures and knew I'd be able to place the remaining artists given their periods and compositions tomorrow at the office. I jotted down a few questions to research before coming to a final appraisal, but my initial assessment of those seven pieces amounted to more than the remainder of my mortgage.

I moved through the room, and every so often, a chill traveled down my spine. He was watching me. In those moments, it felt as if he studied me as intently as I studied the artwork, but in a way that made me feel like prey. I tried to hide the fact I knew he watched me, but my cheeks heated each time those piercing eyes landed on me and caused that unsettling chill.

I worked my way around the room until I arrived at the final painting hanging above the fireplace and close to the devastating man seated behind the desk.

The largest piece in the room, I stared up at the massive oil from where I stood in front of the fireplace. The depiction unnerved me as much as its owner, and I had a difficult time separating my visceral reaction from my academic assessment. It could best be described as dark—tones, medium, subject—the only light on the canvas emanating from the sleeping woman whose life hung in the balance, her body under imminent attack from an evil, leering creature.

And those eyes. The creature's eyes sent another cold shiver through me. The only other light in the painting, they glowed with a sickening lust, their iridescent depths holding malicious intent, a desire bordering on predatory hunger.

Mr. von Dreiss stood from his desk and stepped behind me to my left. His subtle scent—expensive cologne and a hint of brandy—amplified my awareness of his closeness.

"Do you like it?" he asked in a low voice. "This is one of the few pieces I will not be replacing. It has... sentimental value. But it has never been appraised. I would like your professional assessment."

"I..." I swallowed, flustered by the intensity of his proximity and his interest in the disturbing scene. "I'm unfamiliar with the artist, but it's late nineteenth century judging by the condition of the paint and the canvas. Continental, based on the technique and subject." I looked to him for confirmation and found his sea-glass eyes focused on me. He nodded assent, and I turned back to the painting.

"The Continental Romantics painted dark images like this, influenced by medieval folklore. This piece is reminiscent of *The Nightmare*, both in composition—especially the chiaroscuro—and subject. I'd argue this artist achieved a more menacing tone through his suggestion of a humanoid monster rather than a mythological form."

"You have a well-trained eye," he replied in a silken tone. "My family acquired this painting in 1874. It is called *Der Alp*.

"How is your German, Ms. Frye?"

I looked up, and his playful smirk had returned. "Not as good as it used to be," I admitted.

"We will have to fix that," he said and winked.

I worried my legs would give out.

"The... elf?" I asked as I turned back to the painting.

"Yes, although the literal translation from Middle German does not do the meaning justice. *Der Alp* describes a much darker being than what we now think of as an elf. In medieval Germany, the word encompassed many forms of nature demons who seduced women, controlled their dreams, and took them in their sleep, a far broader definition than what arose later and was depicted in *The Nightmare*. The old tales told of beings akin to what you may have heard referred to as an incubus."

"An incubus?" I asked, turning to face him again.

He gave a short nod. "The incubi appear no different than humans, which is perhaps why they are so feared. An incubus cannot be sated by food and drink alone. They experience a more primal hunger, sensual creatures who feed off carnal emotions—lust and sexual pleasure. Without such nourishment, an incubus would die.

"Here, the artist depicts an incubus coming to its victim in the middle of the night. Legends from the time portrayed the incubi as evil creatures, stealing into the homes of unsuspecting women while they slept, haunting their victims' dreams with sexual encounters, and raping them for emotional food."

"It doesn't sound like you agree with that interpretation."

"Well…" He took a step back and reached for his snifter. "They are all stories, no? Fairy tales?"

I watched him as he took a hearty swig of brandy and didn't buy the nonchalant dismissal.

"Well," I said, clearing my throat. "It's getting late, and I finished this room. I need to do research tomorrow morning at the office, but I'll have a report ready for you when I arrive after lunch."

"Ms. Frye," he said gravely and took a step toward me. "This is a partnership, a… conversation if you will, not an assignment. I am looking for a partner in this endeavor, not an employee. I want us to review your findings together, decide what stays and goes. Together."

I swallowed. "Understood, Mr. von Dreiss. Then I look forward to discussing my report with you tomorrow."

"Very good." He nodded and flashed his charming smile. "Auf Wiedersehen, Ms. Frye."

"Auf Wiedersehen, Mr. von Dreiss."

THE FRONT DOOR closed with a click, and I walked down the hall past the foyer to the sitting room, the brandy steadying my frayed nerves. I pulled back the drapes of the bay window, clutching them with a shaking hand, and watched her walk away, the autumn wind blowing through her long chestnut tresses. The subtle sway of her hips entranced me, and I imagined the flush on her pale skin as the cold wind hit her beautiful face.

I had not bet on the appraiser being a woman, much less a woman I found both physically and intellectually alluring. My hunger awakened the moment I laid eyes on her leaning against the doorway of my study.

She drove away, and I closed my eyes, picturing her as she worked, her features shifting while she considered each painting, her hair falling across her shoulder as she tilted her head in contemplation. She smiled, and her light brown eyes lit up with excitement as she furiously wrote in her notebook. My hunger surged at the memory.

She had known I watched her. I tasted the way her desire swelled and body heated in response to my attention. She wanted me as much as I wanted her.

For beauty and passion to accompany knowledge and love of art... A spark of hope lit in my chest. A smoldering ember amid the cold dead emptiness that used to be my heart. Nothing had touched that vacant place in... time did not bear consideration.

Then I pictured her reaction to *Der Alp* and the horror that spread across those delicate features as she took in the gruesome scene. My chest tightened. She had been disgusted, and rightfully so. Without my father's guidance, without his example of my kind's noble potential, my mother's evil ways might have shaped me into the type of incubus people feared, one who only thought of humans as prey, playthings existing solely to feed my gluttonous demonic appetite.

The spark of hope transformed from a blessing into a curse with the reminder of who and what I was—a caged monster capable of draining her with my unchecked need. One night with her would never satisfy my ravenous hunger, which clawed at my insides begging for release.

I needed to stay away, lest my hunger drive me to take unnecessary risks. I needed to stop this compulsion before my feelings progressed any further than lust. I had kept myself in check countless times in the past, determined not to take after my lascivious mother. I held my partners at arm's length, rarely taking them more than once despite their willingness. I fed to survive and nothing more, ignoring my need for companionship let alone love,

35

too afraid of causing the type of destruction the witch so callously wrought.

The temptation of deeper connection was an ever-present curse, and it toyed with me over the years. But I had always resisted, relied on the comfort of my friends and father to soothe at least part of my emptiness. Now, even that solace was gone. My father's slow demise, his gradual starvation after parting from his bond mate, had reached its inevitable conclusion; he had finally succumbed to his fate. Truly alone, I no longer had the strength to fight the lure of Madelyn Frye's enticing mind and body in the face of my desperate loneliness and raging hunger.

The only way to protect her was to bond, but how could such a beautiful woman ever accept a creature like me?

She couldn't. She wouldn't.

I released the curtain and rubbed my hand over my chest, the ache of the emptiness there overwhelming. I promised myself then I would avoid temptation like I had done for countless years and remove myself from a situation that would only result in the pain of her rejection. But as I stared out the window, I couldn't get her face out of my mind.

Madelyn Frye gave me something to look forward to, something to break the monotony of my lonely existence. I knew then, no matter how hard I tried, I wouldn't be able to stay away.

I WOKE UP early the next morning, eager to get started on my report. I hadn't been this excited about a project in years. I looked through several of our in-house reference materials to confirm dates jotted down as estimates and answer my lingering questions. Then I started online research on *Der Alp.*

What little I found about the obscure artist suggested he'd only worked for private patrons, painting on commission as opposed to his own original concepts. Interesting. That meant the von Dreiss family either had *Der Alp* commissioned themselves or purchased the painting from another patron. But which was it? And why did the piece hold such sentimental value for Mr. von Dreiss? No matter the reason, *Der Alp* was rare, and my valuation reflected the novelty.

My desk phone rang.

"Madelyn Frye speaking."

"How was it? What was the house like? Talk fast. I'm on a deadline."

"Hello, Christine. I'm doing well, thanks for asking. How are you today?"

Christine whined like a toddler. I chuckled.

"It was... interesting. The current owner is the former owner's son. The house is, in a word, dusty. No one's lived there in ten years, and it shows. Oh! And those statues out front? Even creepier up close."

Christine snorted.

"Anyway, he's decided to move in, and he's in the process of refurbishing the entire property. As part of the effort, he wants me to help curate an art collection for the house from pieces already there and pieces he's flying over from his family estate in Germany.

"I don't know, Chris. I think we're talking about stupid amounts of money here. Old money. The art and furniture in the one room I saw last night is worth more than my salary. And I'm pretty sure the butler—"

"He has a butler?"

"Yes, he has a butler. I'm pretty sure the butler called him 'baron' last night. Baron!"

"So... he's rich. Is he hot, too?"

"Christine."

"What?"

"Focus."

"I am focused. These are the hard-hitting questions, Mad. The people need to know."

I sighed, closed my eyes, and pinched the bridge of my nose. "Yes, he's hot. In fact, he's devastatingly hot. Now, can we focus?"

"Just making sure."

"I googled his name—Thomas von Dreiss—but didn't come up with much, which is strange for someone with that much art and money. And, apparently, a title. Can you use your reporter skills and see if you can find anything on him? His family, this whole 'baron' thing, their estate?"

"You got it, sis, but after this deadline. My boss is riding my ass. Text me his name and any other info you have, and I'll look into it as soon as I can. Hopefully, there will be pictures."

"God." I chuckled. "You're determined, aren't you?"

"Always. Okay, gotta run. Laters."

"Bye."

After lunch, armed with my final report on the study, I drove to the von Dreiss mansion.

The property looked even worse for wear in the daylight, but Mr. von Dreiss hadn't been kidding about his plans for putting the estate to rights. A veritable fleet of gardeners had descended upon the front lawn, mowing, cutting back weeds, and laying mulch pits around the sculptures. They planted ferns, cut back and winterized roses, and trimmed overgrown branches. Cleaning crews polished lampposts, and scaffolding had been erected on the east side of the mansion where crews sandblasted the stone, scraped chipped paint, and rehung shutters.

I pulled my car into the garage and found it empty, the sexy, silver Porsche missing. Perhaps Mr. von Dreiss had gone out for lunch.

I gathered my things and walked up to the front door, but before I could ring the bell pull, the door swung open to reveal a short, round woman with ruddy cheeks and a stern mouth. She looked me up and down and frowned. Not the welcome I'd expected, but I had my share of cross, German grandmothers—two, to be exact—so her bearing and scowl didn't surprise me.

She wore an apron over her blouse and a skirt that ended below the knee, and her stockinged feet were shoved into sensible, cushioned shoes. Her curly grey hair looked like it had been frozen into place with industrial epoxy. She had a rag draped over her shoulder and held a sheet in her hands.

"Hello," I said.

"Guten Tag," she replied sharply.

"I'm Madelyn Frye." I held out my hand. "From Parker & Sons Real Estate and Consignment."

She eyed my hand with suspicion and then looked back at me. "Ja. Entschuldigung," she said and stepped around me.

I dropped my hand as Fritz appeared in the doorway. "Ach, Ms. Frye. Please, come inside."

He ushered me into a transformed foyer. The sheets had been removed from still-life paintings enclosed in ornate frames, and every inch of the rich, mahogany wood held a newly polished sheen. The chandelier sparkled in the afternoon light coming in through the stained glass and the open door, and an elaborate flower arrangement of autumn blossoms accented by bright oak leaves sat on the entry table beneath its crystal splendor.

"I see you've met Mathilda. Herr von Dreiss is out for the day. You may start with the foyer and the hallway to the study."

I frowned at the announcement of Mr. von Dreiss's absence. Despite my intention the previous evening to not look at this as anything but a job, I'd put extra effort into my appearance that morning. I'd used a flat iron to add waves to my hair, worn my best jeans with a pair of heels that gave my short legs some length and made my ass look fantastic, and made sure not to forget my makeup. What had I been thinking? I needed to get a grip. And yet...

"Will Mr. von Dreiss be returning today? I have the report on the study ready for review."

"Doubtful, madam. He has a very busy schedule."

"Oh. I see," I said, unable to mask my disappointment. "I'll get started then. Thank you, Fritz."

"My pleasure, madam."

That night, back at my condo, I fell into my standard evening routine. I went to my room and changed into a pair of yoga pants, a loose tank top, and a hoodie. I turned the television on in my living room for background noise while I puttered around my kitchen fixing myself a piece of chicken and a salad. Then, I poured myself a glass of wine and sat down on my couch to watch *Pawn Stars*.

I enjoyed my simple dinner while Rick walked the owner of a piece of American pop culture through its history and value. As I sipped my wine, the empty seat next to me on my couch screamed for attention.

Tonight wasn't the first time I'd imagined what life might be like if someone sat there, sipping their wine with me. We'd laugh at Rick's over-simplified description of a piece of art and how he tried to buy the item for cheap. Then we'd have our own discussion of the piece's history and merits.

An ache bloomed in my chest. I took another, deeper drink trying to soothe the pang of loneliness.

I liked my quiet life and had no desire to upset my routine. I enjoyed spending time with my family, walking along the river parkway for exercise, volunteering at the museum, and even sticking to my rigid schedule. But in moments like these, even I had to admit something was missing.

In those quiet moments, I yearned to take comfort in someone who enjoyed the same simple pleasures I did. But at this point in my life, finding someone who shared my interests and wasn't already taken seemed impossible. So, I avoided disappointment; it was one of the reasons I didn't date. Loneliness seemed more manageable than another failure to start, or worse yet a painful breakup.

I threw back the rest of my wine, got up off the couch to take my dishes to the sink, and a vision of Thomas von Dreiss brushing a wave of black hair from his forehead flashed across my mind. Warmth spread through my body at the memory. Here was a man who no doubt shared my passion for art and history, someone who I could discuss a painting with over a glass of brandy, someone I could sit with on the couch while listening to Chopin.

I shook my head, trying to get the image of those gorgeous green eyes out of my head. The last thing I needed was the pain of disappointment, and that was the only place dreams of Thomas von Dreiss led. I pushed him out of my mind, but as I climbed into bed and closed my eyes to sleep, his handsome face kept reappearing in my dreams.

THE NEXT TWO days passed in a similar fashion with no sign of my elusive client. I went to the office in the mornings to do research and prepare my report from the previous day, and then spent the afternoon cataloguing and assessing the art in the freshly cleaned rooms off the east wing hallway of the first floor. Fritz and Mathilda made steady progress, and as the mansion emerged from beneath sheets and years of dust and neglect, I started to see how we could curate the collection, how to group themes and create motifs, what pieces we'd need to fill in the gaps.

The sun set early this time of year, twilight arriving well before the dinner hour or even the normal close of business, and by late Thursday afternoon, I found myself wanting to leave sooner rather than later. The house made me anxious, even more so after moving up to the ballroom on the second floor.

My footsteps echoed through the damp cold of the cavernous space, and the low light of the ancient fixtures cast an eerie glow over the searching eyes of the portraits and the dark romantic landscapes lining the walls. But above all else, I had the distinct feeling of being watched. A presence loomed as I studied the room, and it caused the same, unsettling chill I'd felt the first day in the study. Maybe I just needed some fresh air.

The ballroom sat atop the study on the east end of the mansion and looked out over the lake. I approached the oversized French doors and stood before the newly cleaned glass. The rising moon shone through the naked branches of the oaks climbing out of the rocky descent to the dark waters of Lake Michigan. I reached for the doorknob and wondered when the doors to the magnificent stone balcony had last been opened. I tugged hard, the door resisting my strength until the hinges finally gave way with a screeching whine.

The wind whipped my hair as I stepped through the opening and out onto the balcony. Stone staircases descended on either side of me to the lawn below, strewn with loose rocks and dirt. The scaffolding crept around the northeast corner of the mansion and loomed to my left, casting shadows, while the vast expanse of dense forest extended to the south. I kicked debris out of my path and breathed in the crisp air off the lake, trying to calm my nerves.

The silhouettes of bare branches moved like long gnarled fingers reaching out to grasp something fleeting. The dark waves crashed against the rocky break, and the few remaining leaves clinging to the branches and those tumbling across the lawn rustled in the wind.

I shivered, but not from the wind. An iciness slinked down my spine, except now the sensation felt closer, more insistent. I spun around, looking behind me into the ballroom, scanning the vast, empty space. Nothing but unlit chandeliers, a few of the old fixtures casting their dim glow, and the eyes of the portraits staring back at me. I searched the room a moment longer, sure I'd sensed something, before turning back to the lake.

A man stood at the edge of the rock break facing me. Shadows masked the details of his clothes and face, but by a trick of the moonlight or the light coming from the balcony, his eyes glowed a pale, iridescent green. They focused on me, and I froze like a deer under the stalk of a hungry wolf, the chill stronger than before.

Adrenaline gripped my insides, and I shut my eyes hard. When I opened them again, he'd vanished. I stepped forward, frantic in my search for the man, looking down the stairs of the balcony and out across the lawn leading to the lake, but no one was there.

Adrenaline morphed into fear, and I darted inside. I slammed the creaking door shut and locked it before gathering my notebook and pen. I shoved them into my messenger bag and fled the ballroom, flying down the hallway and stairs, my heart pounding in my chest. I bounded across the foyer and slammed right into Fritz.

"Fritz! Excuse me! I'm so sorry. I… uh… I forgot I have an appointment. I need to go." The words spilled out of me so quickly over my short breath I became dizzy.

"Of course, madam."

I took several deep breaths to calm myself. The urgency to leave and protect myself held fast, but a moment of clarity broke through my panic. Fritz stood next to me; I wasn't alone.

"Did Mr. von Dreiss return this evening?"

"Not that I'm aware of, madam."

I shivered. "Will you walk me to my car, Fritz?"

"Of course, madam."

With Fritz by my side, I hurried to my car in the darkness of the early autumn night. Out of the corner of my eye, the silver outline of another car flashed across my awareness. But without further delay, I jumped into the driver's seat and sped down the driveway, feeling reckless but determined to escape the Witch's House and those lambent green eyes.

MY CELL PHONE went off. Christine. It was early. I'd just left my condo and was headed downtown for work. I hit the answer button and put her on speaker.

"Hey, Chris."

"Hey, Mad. I got that info you wanted."

"Oh yeah?"

"Yeah.

"First off, the guy is rich. And not like Milwaukee rich. Like rich, rich. I had to dig—he's unknown in celebrity circles—but once I started searching outside the typical rags and added 'baron' to the mix? According to an article I found in the *Forbes* archives on European heredity titles, the von Dreiss family has an estimated net worth of four hundred million. And that was in 2005."

"Holy shit!"

"I know. That 'family estate' he mentioned in Germany? Yeah... It's a castle. Southeast of Dresden, right on the Elbe."

"What?"

"You heard me. An actual freaking castle. With like gargoyles and shit."

I blinked slowly. "Castles don't typically have gargoyles, Christine. You're thinking of cathedrals."

"Oh..." Silence. "Really?"

I sighed.

"Anyway, according to German newspapers, the former Baron von Dreiss returned to Dresden in 1990 after Reunification to reclaim the family estate and artwork from the Soviets. Since the family had been outspoken against the Nazis, the German government permitted them to pursue their claims as part of their post-Reunification and hereditary lineage policies. Apparently, the baron spent the better part of twenty years rebuilding the family's art collection. The last appraisal done by Sotheby's in 2009 estimated the Dresden collection worth eighty million."

"Wow."

"Yeah."

"Well, I'm not surprised given the pieces I've seen here and the size of the mansion."

"One more thing, Mad. I tried to find pictures of your hottie, but there is no record of a Thomas von Dreiss in Milwaukee."

"What do you mean?"

"Didn't you say he lived here before? Moved to Germany in 1990? There's no driver's license. No records at any of the local grade schools or high schools—public or private. Nothing. The *Forbes* article mentioned him as heir to the von Dreiss estate, but other than that, it's as if the guy arrived on a plane last week out of nowhere."

"Well, that's… weird."

"Very."

"What about his mother and the house?"

"Not much on that front either. Neither the *Milwaukee Journal* nor the MPD have any records of complaints or charges against the previous owner. But then again, urban legends don't make the front page or warrant police attention. All I can tell you is she died in 2012, and the body was cremated. The obituary said little more than that.

"Look, be careful, okay? There are always records, which makes me think he's hiding something. And you never know with these obscenely rich people—they're eccentric and have freaky fetishes."

I snorted. "Thanks, Chris. I'll call you later, okay?"

"Laters."

That afternoon, I arrived at the mansion unnerved by the events of the previous evening and the revelations from my sister's phone call. I kept telling myself I was overreacting; a trick of the light caused what I'd seen the night before, and an absence of information about Mr. von Dreiss shouldn't condemn him to the conclusions of my overactive imagination. Yet, I couldn't shake the feeling there was more to this story.

After a week of effort, the mansion's entrance and driveway had transformed, the wrought iron gates no longer screamed as they opened, the lawns had been groomed to immaculate cleanliness and artful arrangement, the old gas lamps were polished and functional. The scaffolding on the east side of the mansion had made its way to the south side of the building facing the forest, and the difference between the east and west wings of the façade showed the remarkable results of the restoration efforts.

The modern sculptures had been freed from their overgrowth, and now, fully visible, their depictions of torment and pain created no less of an eerie landscape than before, a persistent reminder of the house's mysterious past.

I walked through the front door.

"Good afternoon, Fritz. Which room will I be working on today?"

"Guten Tag, Ms. Frye. You will be working in the dining room." He paused. "Herr von Dreiss has requested your company for dinner tonight."

I froze as every butterfly in the state of Wisconsin performed aerial tricks in my stomach.

"Oh!"

"Please have the dining room finished by five o'clock so we can prepare it for the evening meal. Dinner is at seven."

"Yes. Yes, of course, Fritz. Thank you. I didn't finish the ballroom last night—there are still a couple pieces left. I'll complete those after the dining room."

"As you wish, madam." Fritz bowed his head, then turned and walked away, leaving me alone in the foyer.

Dinner with Thomas von Dreiss. I'd only met the man once and yet here I was, anticipating the meal like a first date. An absurd idea. He probably just wanted to go over my reports from the week. Yes. That had to be it.

With my head screwed back on straight, ridiculous notions of a date with Thomas von Dreiss banished from my thoughts, I made my way to the dining room and got to work.

The dining room took the better part of the afternoon to catalogue, the large Impressionist landscapes that covered the walls captivating my attention. But eventually, I moved to the ballroom when Mathilda started bustling around the dining room and readying it for dinner, glowering at me as if my very presence offended her.

Alight with its newly repaired fixtures—electricians had arrived at the mansion that morning—the opulent ballroom inspired me with its potential. I imagined the space humming with the energy of a grand fête, a vision of turn-of-the-century splendor. With the right artwork, the ballroom could achieve the inviting and lively ambience needed for such an event. I was jotting down a few final thoughts on the last pieces when Fritz's voice startled me back into the moment.

"Pardon the interruption, Ms. Frye, but Herr von Dreiss would like you to meet him in his study for an aperitif."

I checked my watch. A quarter to seven. I closed my notebook and gave Fritz a nervous smile. "Of course." I put my things in my bag and followed him down the stairs.

"May I take your things, madam?" he asked when we reached the foyer.

"Oh. Uh… Yes, please. Thank you."

"Certainly. Herr von Dreiss is waiting in the study."

I nodded, his formality amplifying my nerves.

As I walked down the hall to the study, the change in the house's energy struck me. The mansion had transformed into a home—alive, lived in, and glowing with a warmth and energy that hadn't existed before. But despite that warmth, the constant suggestion of an unknown presence still followed me wherever I went.

Before entering the study, I did a quick check of my clothes. I smoothed my fitted V-neck sweater and fluffed out my hair. I took a deep breath, rolled my shoulders, and knocked on the door as I pushed it open and stepped through.

Mr. von Dreiss stood behind his desk, a glass of brandy in one hand and papers in the other. He looked up when I entered, and the fall of his wavy black hair combined with the genuine smile at seeing me made my heart flutter. "Hello, Ms. Frye." He tossed the papers on his desk and stepped forward.

He wore a maroon pullover atop a collared shirt with tailored khaki slacks. The color complimented his olive skin and dark hair and accentuated his haunting green eyes. How he managed to look even more handsome than the first day I'd met him boggled my mind.

"Hello, Mr. von Dreiss," I said, my nerves on edge from the intensity of his presence. "Thank you for inviting me to dinner."

"Please. Call me Thomas."

"Thomas, then. And you can call me Madelyn."

"Madelyn." My name on his lips sounded like an illicit promise, and my body reacted with a wave of heat through my core. "I am delighted you agreed to join me for dinner. I apologize for my absence this week, but several shipments from my estate in Germany arrived, and I needed to ensure everything was settled at the warehouse."

"No worries. Fritz has been very welcoming and helpful. I've prepared reports for each room. I'm sure you're eager to go over them. Oh! I left them in my bag. I'll go get them."

His lush lips quirked in an amused smile that reached his eyes and made my knees weak. "All work and no play is no way to live."

I stared at him, speechless in my confusion.

"I do hope we can discuss your reports, but that is not why I invited you to dinner. I invited you to dinner because I enjoyed our time together the other night and wanted to get to know you better."

Don't faint. Dinner with a sexy, millionaire baron is totally normal.

"Oh."

Brilliant reply, Mad. So eloquent.

He chuckled. "You seem surprised."

"Well, I uh..." I swallowed. "I mean..."

"Can I offer you a drink?"

My shoulders descended from their perch near my ears, and I sighed with relief. "Yes, please."

He walked over to the sideboard and poured a finger of brandy for me.

We both stepped toward one another, and when he handed me the glass, his fingers brushed against mine and a charge passed between us. I looked up into eyes so bright and filled with heat they almost glowed. They reminded me of the vision I'd had the other night in the ballroom. I blinked hard, surprised at myself for the fantasy I'd concocted. His gorgeous—and normal—sea-glass eyes stared back.

"Thank you." I brought the glass to my lips and smiled like a lovesick teenager.

The smooth caramel and banana flavors coated my mouth, warmed my throat and belly, and calmed my nerves. Ah, liquid courage. And not just any liquid courage. I hadn't had brandy like this... ever.

"This is delicious."

He tilted his head in acknowledgement, and then we stood, sipped our drinks, and furtively eyed one another.

"Tell me about yourself, Madelyn."

"What would you like to know?"

"Everything," he replied, the sincerity of his answer evident in his searching eyes. His lip twitched before he continued. "But you can start with how you came to work in estate consignment."

I nodded. "I went to school out east for art history, much to the chagrin of my parents, who didn't think I'd be able to get a job after graduation with such an 'indulgent' degree." I chuckled. "But I love art and couldn't be swayed, so I double majored in education. I could always come back and teach if nothing else."

"Smart woman."

My heart warmed at the compliment. "I fell in love with the program. I stayed on and got my master's. I even spent a year in Germany studying in Berlin."

He cocked an eyebrow. "Really?"

I smiled, fighting a blush. "Yes, but that was almost twenty years ago now, back when my German wasn't so rusty, so don't get any ideas."

His eyes twinkled with mischief.

"I lucked out when I moved back to Milwaukee—the new art museum addition had been completed the year before, and they were hiring. I got an internship under one of the curators, which opened a lot of doors for me. It's how I met Mr. Parker. He routinely reached out to the museum with pieces he acquired from the estates he handled. Apparently, I impressed him with my assessments, and since I wanted a permanent position where I could make enough money to buy a house... Well, here we are."

He crooked a smile. "Here we are."

"Your dinner is ready, sir," Fritz announced from the doorway.

"Wonderful. Thank you, Fritz." Thomas reached for my glass. I handed the snifter to him, and he placed both on the sideboard before gesturing toward the door. "Shall we?"

I moved past him, and as we stepped into the hall, he placed his hand on the small of my back. My body stiffened with nervous tension at the unexpected desire that blossomed from that small gesture.

He leaned forward, close enough that his warm breath caressed my neck, and I could smell the brandy on his breath. "Relax, meine Liebe. It's only dinner."

My head snapped up, and he winked at me over a charming, wicked smile. I blushed hard, but smiled back, and forced myself to relax as we crossed the foyer to the dining room.

I TRIED TO put distance between us, protect her, but Madelyn's allure was too powerful to deny. I knew the moment I saw her standing on my ballroom balcony I couldn't stay away much longer. I wanted to be near her again if only to share a conversation. I could no longer keep the overwhelming loneliness at bay in the face of this woman whose brilliant appreciation for art and simple beauty tempted long forgotten hopes. But I wouldn't pursue her. I couldn't risk the pain of rejection when she inevitably discovered my secret. A dinner and our professional relationship would have to suffice.

We entered the dining room, and I led her to the spot next to the head of the table and pulled out her chair. She looked at me with surprise, then lowered her eyes as if embarrassed by my gesture, endearing her to me even more. Had no one ever treated her like the treasure she was?

I took my seat at the head of the table, pleased with the elegant setting Mathilda had laid out for us.

Fritz appeared out of nowhere to pour the wine, and I stared at Madelyn's wide eyes as she watched the expensive red trickle into my mother's crystal.

I lifted my glass and swirled its contents beneath my nose. Notes of spice and currant wafted from the rich liquid. Perfection.

"To art," I said, and she lifted her glass to meet mine. I held her gaze as she replied, "To art."

Madelyn's eyes sparkled with surprised delight as she tasted the robust cabernet, and I vowed to serve her anything to elicit such a reaction again.

She set her glass down, folded her napkin in her lap, and turned to me. "So, Thomas. How long did you live in Milwaukee before you and your father moved to Germany?"

I smirked at her coy question.

"I'm forty-nine," I replied, giving her the answer she was after. The number was a certain sort of truth.

She turned her head away and smiled sheepishly. When she turned back, she straightened in her chair and arched an eyebrow.

"You don't look forty-nine."

"Good genes."

She laughed, and the light and airy sound warmed my chest and relaxed my tense shoulders.

Fritz entered with the soup and set the individual, porcelain tureens before us.

"How beautiful!" Madelyn exclaimed with genuine interest. "I should have known you'd have a collection of Dresden Porcelain."

"It is a form of art, is it not?"

Her smile reached her light brown eyes. "Yes. Absolutely."

"My family brought this set over when the house was first built in 1880."

She stared down at the tureen with awe and a new appreciation. She looked back at me with joy in her expression. "I've always found Dresden Porcelain a beautiful art form. Both my grandmothers had a set, and I used to pretend we were royalty when I was a little girl. I made my dolls sit for tea."

She looked down as a blush reached her cheeks. She fidgeted with her spoon and swallowed, then looked back up at me with a nervous smile.

"Speaking of which…" She arched her brow. "That first day, Fritz called you *Baron* von Dreiss."

I chuckled. Sometimes Fritz's nostalgia got the best of him. "Yes, technically, I am a baron, but hereditary titles lost meaning with the founding of the Republic in 1919. My family maintained its estate and lands and the name. The title is still passed down through a male heir, but beyond that it is merely tradition."

"I see. But what about your father? I thought he lived with you in Germany."

I stared at my wine, needing to focus on anything but the pain stabbing the empty place where my heart should be at the mention of my father. I twirled the glass by its stem. "My father died six months ago."

"Oh, Thomas. I'm so sorry."

I raised my eyes, not wanting to cause her any distress, and managed a smile. "It's all right. You didn't know." I sipped my wine and tried my best not to let on how much the impact of losing my only remaining family, my only lasting connection, affected me. "He lived a long and full life." I huffed out a breath. "I am surprised he survived as long as he did. Life was hard for him after my mother died. He couldn't live with her—couldn't stand to be around her, in fact—but he needed her, in his own way. A few times a year, depending, they met here or in Germany. And when that ended... It was only a matter of time."

"Is that why you moved here?"

I nodded. "The Dresden estate is beautiful. You would adore it. So much art and history. But the castle is too big for one person. I have no family of my own, and without my father, it became too much. Too many memories." I swirled my glass again, for a moment losing myself to the past.

"But this house..." I looked around the dining room, noticing the impressive transformation in only a week. "This house and its art have languished far too long. I needed a change of pace and a new project to occupy my time."

She gave me an encouraging smile. "Well, there's no shortage of work to do here. I hope the project brings you the distraction and comfort you're looking for."

I acknowledged her kind words with a tilt of my head, even though I knew the project wouldn't fill the void. I had traded the emptiness of a castle for the emptiness of a mansion.

Loneliness had plagued me for as long as I could remember, and it had only gotten worse since my father died. He'd become my best friend in many ways, the only person who understood our circumstances, our shared history, and what I faced. Incubi and succubae were few and far between, and although we crossed paths over the years, I had forged no lasting relationships with others of my kind, put off by my mother's family and reticent to bond after living through my parent's failed noble pairing. Years of fleeting friendships with humans left me raw, losing each one to their numbered years after living only a fraction of my own. Eventually, I stopped pursuing such connections, finding solitude easier than suffering through more loss. But without genuine connection, life became tiresome, an especially daunting prospect for an immortal.

After my father's death, I threw myself into planning the effort, trying in vain to focus on anything but my loss. But restoring the estate would only provide a few months of relief from the gaping hole that dominated my life.

A life filled with happiness and love is possible. She is your hope.

I pushed the thoughts aside; I couldn't afford hope.

"And don't forget the sculpture garden in the front yard," she innocently continued, oblivious to my maudlin thoughts.

I groaned at the mention of the hideous display on my lawn, my mother's sadistic legacy made manifest in her selection of modern sculpture. The last thing I needed was to preserve another reminder of how she'd reveled in torture and pain to serve her own pleasure.

"Trust me, I have not forgotten about that eyesore." She suppressed a laugh. "I am in talks with several art museums to donate the pieces, but as you know, that takes time."

Madelyn took a spoonful of soup before giving me a mischievous smile. "You've heard the rumors, right?"

I raised an eyebrow, taunting her. "Why don't you tell me?" I had an idea to what she referred but wanted to hear the ridiculous stories from her lips.

"People call this place the 'Witch's House.'"

I huffed out a chuckle. "Well, she certainly was a witch," I said ruefully, and Madelyn's brow rose at my harsh admission. "But not the flying on broomsticks kind," I added with a wry smile.

She winced. "I shouldn't speak ill of the dead. Especially your mother. I'm sorry."

I waved my hand, dismissing her concern. "The baroness and I did not have a great relationship. Most of the time we had *no* relationship." I lifted my glass. "By all means. Let's hear the rumors."

She gave me a wary look, but then sipped her wine and leaned forward as if sharing an illicit secret. "Local legend has it that you and your father died in a tragic accident. That you fell off the bluff into the lake and drowned." I raised an eyebrow, stifling my mirth at the ludicrous tale. "But some say it wasn't an accident. Some say the witch killed you both herself—"

I burst out laughing. I couldn't help myself.

"Oh, that's rich," I said through my snickers. I dabbed my eyes with the corner of my napkin, and then sighed as I regained composure. "My mother was an absolute bitch, but she would never have dared cross my father, or me. Instead, she drove us away with her insufferable antics. And, as you can see, I am sitting here in one piece."

She laughed along with me, and the tension left her shoulders.

"The story is outrageous, isn't it?" she said. I took a spoonful of soup. "But you know teenagers— always looking for an excuse to cause trouble. Run into a yard on a dare. Tempt a witch out of hiding."

We laughed together and that connection filled the hole in my chest for the briefest moment.

"There were other rumors, you know."

"Oh?"

She nodded with an amused smile. "Some say the sculptures are the grave markers of past lovers. That the witch who lived here tempted men into her home, never to be seen again."

My body tensed, and my blood turned to ice.

She looked at me with a playful smile, no doubt expecting the same reaction as when she'd suggested I'd drowned. I laughed along with her, forcing a smile onto my face even as my stomach roiled with thoughts of my mother. I took a long drink of wine.

The tacky sculptures may not have been grave markers, but my mother's reckless dalliances and malicious use of her powers were far from rumor. She enthralled any visitors she found intriguing and fed on them with reckless abandon. She curated tormented victims like the collection of sculptures that dotted my front lawn. She had no care for her human lovers and found perverse enjoyment in using a person until they turned into a sexual thrall, compelled and eager to give of themselves until they knocked on death's door.

Her indulgences grew more wicked with each passing year, and she flaunted her victims in front of my father and me, her behavior a constant reminder of the worst of our kind. Disgusting beast.

"May I clear your places?" Fritz's interruption saved me from my thoughts and the conversation. Able to breathe again, I shook off the distasteful memories and focused on Madelyn, which brought a smile to my face and spread warmth through my body.

"Thank you, Fritz."

As Fritz cleared our dishes, I looked at Madelyn with intent, wanting to engage her every moment we had and eager to change the subject off my parents.

"Tell me, Madelyn. What do you think of the house so far? The art. I'm curious to hear your impressions."

We spent the evening discussing the house, art, and history. Her passion for art ran as deep as mine. We talked about her years at the museum, my father and my restoration of the Dresden estate, her love of *Pawn Stars*, my love of piano, and our mutual heritage. She hadn't visited her family in Germany in years and wanted to go back. I wanted to take her. The easy and balanced conversation filled my emptiness with laughter, comfort, and joy.

The missing piece of myself sat across from me, something I had never dreamed possible, and now that I found her, I never wanted to let her go. What had I done to deserve this woman walking into my life? Was this my chance to find fulfillment and happiness after all this time?

She lifted the back of her hand to her lips to stifle a yawn, and I looked at the clock. Ten. It might as well have been midnight the way her yawn broke the spell that had allowed me to feel for a night.

THE MORE TIME I spent with Thomas, the more comfortable and natural our conversation, like we'd known each other for years. He listened to my impressions of his collection with an enthusiasm and curiosity I hadn't experienced before, even with my colleagues. Mr. Parker only cared that I did my job and made him a hefty commission, uninterested in the knowledge I used to accomplish the task. The dialogue with Thomas went both ways, and I found myself as keen to hear what he had to say as sharing my own thoughts on the pieces.

Then the conversation turned, and we talked about our lives and interests, and a rapport blossomed between us beyond any professional connection. Here was a man whose company I could enjoy, who I could relax with on my couch while drinking a glass of wine, who I could share my nights with...

I lost track of time; I could have talked to Thomas all night. But it had been a long day, and fatigue overtook my desire to remain in his presence. I yawned.

"I've kept you too late, meine Liebe," he said. "Time to go. We don't want you falling asleep behind the wheel."

My dear. My heart warmed at the term of endearment. I'd made a promise to not put myself in a situation where I'd be disappointed, but I knew that battle had been lost after tonight.

I stifled another yawn. "You're probably right."

Thomas got up, and with manners one might expect from a baron, pulled out my chair and held out his arm. I rose, took his arm, and he walked me to the foyer. Fritz waited with my coat and bag in hand, and before I could decline, Thomas opened the front door and offered to walk me to my car.

"I think you need a new car," he said, voice droll as we approached my beat-up Volkswagen.

I chuckled. "Bite your tongue. You'll hurt its feelings."

He laughed, a deep sound from his belly that made my toes curl. When I spun around to thank him for the lovely evening, he stepped closer, and a frisson of heat streaked through my body.

"Thank you for sharing dinner with me, Madelyn."

"Thank you for having me, Thomas."

Something about his bearing and his eyes penetrated my soul, awakening my senses and drawing me to him. I stood transfixed by his intoxicating presence. I wanted this man in ways that defied rational thought. He intimidated and intrigued me in equal parts.

He crooked a smile and brushed the hair from my face. The air between us sizzled with anticipation, desire flying across the short distance.

My body came alive under the intensity of his closeness. I licked my lips, chapped from the dry cold, and stared into his haunting eyes.

My heart leapt as he leaned closer. He cupped my cheek and lowered his perfect, lush mouth to mine. My eyes closed automatically, and a whisper of touch brushed my eager lips. Electric pleasure surged through me unlike anything I'd experienced in my life. And as he pressed his lips against mine, the feeling swelled, and my body melted with desire. In that moment, I would have given anything to him, the intensity of his touch claiming me as his own.

He pulled away after only a moment, and his sudden absence left me stunned, eyes still closed, and body aching with pleasure and longing for more.

When I opened my eyes, his shone bright with desire and amusement. He smiled then and lowered his hand from my face.

"Sweet dreams, meine Liebe."

He turned and walked away as I squeaked out, "Bye."

THROUGHOUT THE WEEKEND, my thoughts drifted to Thomas, our dinner, and that mind-blowing kiss. I promised myself I wouldn't fall for him or dare hope he might be interested in me. I refused to set myself up to be let down. Still, I daydreamed about sipping brandy with him while we discussed art, our easy conversations, and the way his kiss set my body aflame with desire. I was falling for Thomas, and no matter what I tried I couldn't rein in the urgent craving to be near him again. Luckily for my heart, my work at the mansion was almost complete. I'd move on to other tasks, and once Thomas settled into his new life in Milwaukee, he'd no doubt find friends and women more suitable for a baron.

The uneventful weekend passed as many of my weekends did, relaxing and spending time with family. I hung out at my sister's house on Saturday and took my nephew out to practice driving, nearly giving myself a heart attack in the process. On Sunday, I visited my parents for lunch and football.

I arrived home later than planned, staying at my parents' house for dinner after my sister stopped by without warning, started pulling things out of the fridge, and ordered everyone to sit. I unlocked my condo, threw my purse on the end table, and walked into the kitchen to pour myself a glass of chardonnay, determined to enjoy the last vestiges of my weekend. I took my wine into my bedroom to change.

I threw my clothes in the hamper, and as I rummaged through my drawers for a clean camisole, a chill traveled down my spine, the same other-worldly sensation I'd felt at the von Dreiss mansion. I tried to shake off the unsettling feeling but couldn't. So, as I braided my hair, I walked over to my bedroom window and looked out. Bright streetlights illuminated empty sidewalks, and the occasional car crawled down the otherwise quiet side street.

I shook my head. My imagination had been working overtime lately. I grabbed my wine and made my way back to the living room and my place on the couch.

I started nodding off only halfway through the first episode of *Pawn Stars*, so I turned off the TV, put my empty glass in the sink, and crawled into bed.

An autumn breeze wafted through the crack I'd left in the window, but warmed by my fluffy down comforter, I welcomed the cool night air as it danced across my bare arms and neck. I drifted in and out of consciousness, lingering in the space between wakefulness and sleep where dreams pervade conscious thought.

Something weighed down the foot of my bed, and a warm presence started to climb up my body. The chill returned, but this time a tingling sensation accompanied it, dancing across my skin and pooling between my legs. I didn't need to look up to know the source of the warmth.

Thomas.

He crawled up the length of my bed and hovered over me. A hint of his expensive cologne filled my nostrils, and as he lowered himself to me, his forearms on either side of my head, the faint smell of brandy combined with his cologne to create a scent undeniably his. The breeze from the window caressed my exposed skin, and his lips brushed feather-light kisses across my collarbone, making me shiver.

"What are you doing here?" I whispered through sleep, barely awake even in my dream.

"I am here to make you come, Madelyn."

I moaned, aroused by the sound of his voice and his promise. I turned my head, inviting him to my neck, which he tended to with soft lips.

"Would you like that?" he whispered and dragged his tongue along the ridge of my ear.

"Yes. Please, Thomas. Yes."

His lips ventured down past my collarbone, and he pushed my camisole up my torso to expose my breasts. My nipples hardened from the cold air and the anticipation of his touch. I squirmed with his mouth so close to my sensitive flesh, but before I could beg for his mouth, his tongue circled the tight bud, and I groaned. My hands flew to his hair, tangling themselves in the silky waves as he tortured my nipple with gentle, sensual strokes. He made his way to the other one, and the alternating cool breeze to his warm mouth had me writhing under his touch.

He kissed his way down my stomach, and his hands caressed my sides before landing on my hips. I released his hair, fisting the sheets instead, desire coursing through my body in waves centered between my legs. Anticipation hooked me like a drug, and I was high on the prospect of what came next. He squeezed my hips as he placed one last kiss right above my landing strip. Then his hands moved to my thighs, kneading them. I looked down to see him staring at me, first at my sex, open to him now as he spread my legs, and then my face. His eyes glowed with an iridescent light as his whispered, "So schön."

He lowered his head and swept his tongue along the seam of my sex, from my entrance to my pulsing clit, and I sighed aloud in pure, carnal bliss. He stroked his tongue against me, taking his time with languid laps and swirls. Slow, sensual ministrations, driving my lust to a peak without frantic movement, but with deliberate sexual prowess. He drove me mad with each relentless stroke, and when his fingers penetrated my entrance, I cried out, nearly pushed over the edge by the fullness they created inside me. Finally, he closed his mouth over my clit, sucking and flicking with his tongue as his two fingers penetrated me with tender thrusts and sealed my fate.

My orgasm ripped through me. I called his name as I clung to the sheets, my body convulsing in the most powerful release of my life. Over and over, my body shook with pleasure as he drew even more from my body, eventually waking me from the erotic dream. I opened my eyes, still coming down from the aftermath of my orgasm…

And there he was, between my legs, wicked smile across swollen lips, and eyes glowing like lanterns, a pale, iridescent green.

I sat up with a start, scooting back to my headboard, and clutched the sheets. I shut my eyes hard, pushing loose pieces of sweat-soaked hair off my face. When I opened my eyes, no one was there. My hand fell to my heaving chest as I tried to get air into my lungs. My stomach leapt into my chest as fear, excitement, and the last vestiges of my orgasm sent conflicting sensations through my body.

What had just happened? I lifted my hand to my forehead. It was clammy and a bead of sweat trickled down the side of my face. I ran my fingers along my collarbone and down my chest, tracing the path of kisses Thomas had left in my dream. My body still tingled from the sensations of his touch. I reached down and slid my hand into my underwear. I was wet. Soaked. I slumped back down into my bed and pulled the covers up to my chin.

I stared at the ceiling and sighed long and slow, disconcerted yet undeniably aroused. I'd heard of lucid dreams before, but never experienced anything like that.

Despite the adrenaline, exhaustion hit me like a wall. I needed sleep. I was as physically drained as if I'd run a marathon, and weariness won out against racing thoughts and emotions. I'd been daydreaming about Thomas all weekend, and that realistic dream was just a natural reaction to having him on my mind. Right?

I DROVE TO the mansion Monday afternoon wondering how I'd be able to have a conversation with Thomas after my dream the previous night. I blushed remembering the vivid fantasy and how I'd had the best orgasm of my life from a dream! I shook my head and tried to clear my mind of that gorgeous man between my legs. I needed to focus on work, finish this job, and move on with my life. Stop lusting after a man so far out of my league it wasn't funny.

Despite my exhaustion from the night before, I threw myself into the remaining rooms on the second floor. I'd fallen back asleep almost immediately after waking up in that sweat-soaked state but struggled to open my eyes in the morning when my alarm went off. I was so tired, like I hadn't slept at all. But I needed to go over the reports with Thomas, and I still had rooms to finish cataloguing and appraising, so I braced myself for a long day.

About an hour into the first room, that telltale chill wandered down my spine. I spun around to find Thomas leaning against the door frame, arms folded across his chest watching me.

"Oh! Thomas."

"Hello," he replied with a smile.

"I was just finishing up this bedroom. Did you need something?"

He dropped his arms and shoved his hands into his pockets. "You," he replied easily.

I couldn't peel my eyes away from his lips as he formed the word. My entire body tingled with arousal thinking about where those lips had been the night before in my dream.

"I… uh…"

"I hoped to discuss your reports this afternoon."

"Oh! Yes! Of course," I fumbled. "I'll be down in ten minutes. I want to finish up a couple notes on this last piece."

He tilted his head in acknowledgement, pushed off the frame, and walked away.

My shoulders relaxed, and I took a deep breath to settle my nerves—and hormones—before returning to my notes.

I LOOKED UP from my desk when Madelyn appeared at my door. Finally. I needed to be close to her again, especially after last night.

"Is now a good time?" she asked.

"Yes. Please, come in." I leaned back in my chair.

She carried a stack of labeled manila envelopes, and as she approached my desk, her hands shook even though she exuded an eager confidence about her work. Perhaps last night had been as earth-shattering for her as it had been for me.

"Each folder contains my report on a different room. But before we go through the details, I have an overall concept for the house I'd like to share."

I smiled, excited to hear what this brilliant woman had concocted. "I am all ears."

"I think we should curate themes. I know your mother's taste leaned… eclectic—" I huffed out a snort at the understatement. "—but the rooms *do* have distinct feels to them. The study, for example, has a decidedly masculine feel. It reminds me of a room in a Victorian-era country estate. The leather, the colors, even the piano. Refined, yet masculine. The artwork we choose to decorate the walls should complement that aesthetic.

"Similarly, the ballroom, dining room, and the bedrooms each have their own qualities, a certain ambiance, and we can select a theme, maybe even a period, that reflects the tone of each and then organize the art you'd like to keep along those lines, augmenting with pieces from your personal collection as needed."

Her eyes lit up as she described her plan, and she spread the envelopes out on my desk, each one labeled with a room and its theme. "So organized." I flipped one open and leafed through the papers.

"I take my job seriously. And given the amount of money you're paying my boss to do this work, I think a little organization is in order."

I looked up at sparkling eyes and an eager, hopeful smile. In that moment, I would have given her anything to ensure she looked at me like that again. "I think it's a brilliant idea."

"Excellent! I knew you'd like it. We can start with your study since you spend most of your time here."

"All right."

She edged closer to my desk to walk me through the papers, and her nearness drove me to distraction. I tried to pay attention to what she said, but images of my hands on her thighs kept flashing through my mind.

She paused, looking around the room as if considering what she'd just described, and nodded to herself through a yawn. "Excuse me," she said with an embarrassed smile.

I couldn't prevent a knowing grin from taking over my face. "Didn't sleep well last night?"

Her eyes went wide. Part of me wanted her to know what we shared last night had actually happened, albeit through a dream, and that I could give her even more of what we enjoyed in the flesh. But the shame of what I was and the guilt at what I had done without her understanding stopped me.

I hadn't been able to get Madelyn out of my mind after our dinner, and my hunger overpowered my restraint. The time had come; I needed to feed, and the thought of taking anyone but Madelyn made me sick. So, I did something I promised myself I would never do and invaded her dreams, no better than that monster in *Der Alp*. Yes, I had asked permission—I would have begged—but I didn't need to. I had tasted her desire. She had been willing, eager even. She had said yes, pleading with me to make her come, and I couldn't deny myself any longer.

I hadn't fed through a dream in more than a century, and last night I devoured Madelyn's emotions like a man starved. Her desire and pleasure, so vibrant and genuine, nourished me in ways the one-night stands I normally used to feed couldn't touch. Her orgasm overwhelmed me, and my power surged in response. I felt strong, healthy, and virile, the difference between a man who ate fast food and a man fed gourmet meals prepared with love. The quality and satisfaction didn't compare.

I could never hurt her. I could never take anything she wasn't willing to give. But I had succumbed to my hunger and allowed it to drive me to feed through a dream despite her ignorance of my true nature. My weakness disgusted me; my guilt overwhelmed me. If she knew the truth, she'd run, and I needed her at my side—her partnership, her conversation, her passion. I didn't want this to end and go back to my lonely, solitary existence. I had to tell her or let her go. There was no in between.

"I... No. I'm fine. I didn't have enough coffee this morning, that's all." Her cheeks flamed red, and I knew exactly what crossed her mind. I hadn't been able to focus my own thoughts on anything but what we had done either.

"We can remedy that." I smiled at her, gently, wanting to ease her discomfort.

I called Fritz for coffee and allowed her to keep her secret as we finished discussing plans for the study.

THE WEEK CONTINUED much like Monday with me working on the upstairs bedrooms for about an hour after lunch and then joining Thomas in his study to prepare our grand plan. With each passing day, our conversations grew more comfortable, often veering off topic into stories about ourselves. The hours slipped by in his company, and I stayed later than necessary to share a brandy before leaving. I'd become attached to Thomas von Dreiss, and I wanted him to kiss me again more than anything in the world. But he hadn't made a move since the dinner we shared, and I decided that perhaps the attraction only went one way.

By Thursday afternoon, only one room remained. I sat in Thomas's study, not wanting the day to end and be faced with the final hours of the job and my final hours with him. The prospect of not being able to talk to Thomas about art and enjoy his company weighed on my heart. Our inevitable parting was going to result in the exact disappointment I'd wanted to avoid. I didn't want to go back to my routine. For the first time, my average, safe life no longer satisfied me. Thomas and this job had reinvigorated me, and the thought of letting go of the source of my new zest for life didn't sit well.

How had I fallen for this man after only two weeks? I knew virtually nothing about his mysterious past, yet I did know him. I knew his passion for art, music, and history. I knew his quiet, contemplative nature. I knew his refined taste. I knew he was gentle and lonely; I'd seen the sadness in his eyes. And despite the short amount of time we'd spent together, my feelings for him were no less real.

I stood and walked over to him, seated behind his desk, both to finish explaining my vision for the ballroom and wanting to be close to him one last time. I leaned over and pointed at the diagram I'd drawn on the back of the manila envelope and froze when his hand started to travel up and down the

84

back of my leg in a gentle yet possessive caress. My voice caught as desire and relief surged through me. He ran his hand up and down as if it was the most natural gesture in the world, and I lost my train of thought. I turned my face to meet his and stared into those sea-glass pools.

"You must know I admire you, Madelyn," he said, and my heart soared.

Speechless, I looked down at him as he looked up at me, his eyes searching mine for some confirmation I shared the sentiment.

"I don't want our time together to come to an end. Not professionally. Not personally."

I'm not sure what came over me, but for once in my life, I took a chance. I ignored the fact we'd only known each other for a brief time. I ignored the questions I had about the house and his past. I shored up every vestige of bravery I had, and as I lifted my hand it shook, but I didn't stop. I brushed the lock of black, wavy hair that had fallen across his forehead out of the way.

"I don't want that either," I whispered.

Thomas closed his eyes, shivering at my touch, and leaned into my hand. He gently grasped my wrist, and his affectionate touch humbled me.

He opened his eyes. "Let me take you out tomorrow night after we finish here. I want to treat you to a proper date."

I blinked, and he smiled. "Yes, I want to date you, Madelyn." He turned my hand over and kissed my palm. "I also thought you might be interested in a job curating the von Dreiss family collection. It is vast. What you have seen here is a mere fraction of the artwork I own. You would be responsible for arranging storage for the collection, lending pieces to museums, curating what is on display. I cannot think of a more perfect person for the job."

He stood, then, and took my shoulders in his hands. He loomed over me, even with my heels. "I hope you will consider my offer. I hope you will consider me." He ran his thumb across my cheek. "I am going to kiss you, Madelyn."

The words hit hard, the intensity of his voice coupled with the phrasing that took me back to the night of my dream. He wanted me, wanted us, and despite my trepidation, I wanted him with every fiber of my being.

His warm breath filled the space between our lips and caressed my face. He threaded his long fingers into my hair, and as I placed tentative hands on his chest, he lowered his soft lips to mine. He took my top lip between his, and then the bottom, as if testing the feel and connection between us. The heat in my core ignited into a raging fire. He transformed me into a fountain of lust from the mere touch of his lips. His hand tilted my head back as if sensing the rush of desire, taking it as an invitation to my mouth. He parted my lips with his tongue, now kissing me in earnest for the first time, slowly, reverently, as if time had stopped and we were the only beings left in the world.

His kiss was passionate without being frantic. He explored my mouth with gentle yet desperate sensuality. Slow, deliberate, and filled with ardor, I melted into the kiss, following his lead, responding to the demands of his lips and his tongue. I wrapped my arms around his neck as he kissed me, holding on to him for purchase, my knees weak from him worshipping my mouth.

My reaction to Thomas went far beyond lust. My body, aflame with need so strong it almost hurt, drew closer to his. I wanted to press myself against him, feel every inch of his body against mine. But then he pulled away, and my body rebelled against his absence. A strangled sigh escaped me, and the sound snapped me back into reality.

I stepped back and swallowed, trying to regain composure, and knowing if I stayed too close, I'd lose my resolve. Our eyes locked, he dropped his hand from my hair and took my hand. He brought my fingers to those velvety lips of his and kissed their tips.

"I have been lonely for so long, Madelyn. And these past two weeks, your presence has filled the hole in my heart with happiness and made my life complete."

Before I could respond to his unexpected profession, his phone rang.

He glanced down. "My lawyer in Germany," he mumbled. He frowned and dropped my hand. "It's late there. This must be about the shipment arriving tomorrow. I need to take this."

He turned back to me, took my face in both his hands, and pressed a kiss to my forehead. "Until tomorrow, meine Liebe. Wiedersehen." Then he picked up his phone and held it to his ear. "Hallo, Herr Müller. Ja, ich habe die von Ihnen gesendeten Unterlagen erhalten..."

I stood there for a moment, reeling, trying to process what just happened. The man of my dreams had offered me a job and then kissed me as if I was his entire world. The situation was so outside my comfort zone as to be laughable. Upending my safe routine with a new job and a new relationship. The complications of combining work with pleasure, especially if the relationship ended. These were things I'd never consider, the prospects far too messy and fraught with risk.

Messy, yes, but also exhilarating.

I blinked hard, surprised at the excitement that shot through me, then swallowed. On autopilot, I gathered my notebook and walked out of the study.

I FINISHED THE final bedroom the next day, earlier than planned, and stood in the hallway, looking up and down its length and imagining what the house would look like once Thomas arranged the art and furniture the way we discussed. The house had transformed in the past two weeks from an overgrown, dust covered Witch's House, into Thomas's home—a warm, inviting space, sparkling under gleaming, refurbished light fixtures with manicured lawns, freshly painted eaves, and polished wood.

My gaze landed on the door at the far end of the hallway opposite the ballroom. I'd asked about the room several days ago, but Fritz said to ignore it. He must not have finished cleaning it yet. Surely, he'd cleaned the room by now. I had time, so I took the initiative to inspect the additional room.

I opened the door and immediately realized I'd entered Thomas's bedroom. The suite smelled of his expensive cologne and clean linens. The scent alone made me shiver with need.

He'd decorated the room in deep blues with amethyst accents, dark mahogany furniture that matched the woodwork of the house, and a large leather chaise, giving it a masculine yet overtly sensual appeal. An oversized canvas hung on the wall opposite the massive four-poster bed and stuck out like a sore thumb. A pastoral scene with horses— so not Thomas, and so not in his bedroom— probably a vestige of his mother's décor. He'd likely want to be rid of the sedate Impressionist vista and replace it with something matching the boudoir aesthetic, something Baroque, perhaps.

The massive California King dominated the room with its midnight blue canopy hanging from thick posts. The curtains facing the door were tied back to reveal a rich, damask bedspread and a heap of silk-covered pillows. My lusty brain imagined what Thomas and I might do among those sheets.

I scanned the dressing chair, end table, wardrobe—all antiques in perfect condition—and then walked around the end of the bed. A door on the opposite wall led to an ensuite bath, and to its left…

I froze.

A painting of Thomas hung on the wall, obscured from the entrance by the curtains on the far side of the bed. He lay sprawled on a chaise lounge, naked from the waist up with one arm stretched overhead, the other draped along his side. He wore late nineteenth century breeches, and they sat low on his hips, revealing a trail of dark hair that started at his muscled abdomen and led below the partially opened button flap. His feet were bare, one foot flat on the chaise, propping up his bent leg, the other leg extended. His silky black hair was longer than it was now, tied back at the nape of his neck. It fell rakishly across his forehead, loose waves framing the handsome features of his chiseled face. His sculpted body looked reminiscent of a Greek god, lounging idly, and sexual energy poured off the canvas.

But the thing I couldn't stop staring at were his eyes. They glowed a pale, iridescent green like I'd seen in the distance the night on the balcony, like I'd seen for a brief moment after he first kissed me, and like I'd seen in the dream after he finished taking me with his mouth. Even more disconcerting was that they matched, almost perfectly, the eyes of *Der Alp*.

There was no trace of evil in those eyes. Instead of a malevolent hunger, Thomas's eyes shone with longing and need. Above his familiar, lush lips, parted and turned down in a slight frown, the artist had captured and portrayed eyes that bespoke of deep desire and passion, but at the same time a pensive vulnerability. A pang of empathy washed over me, breaking through my shock, because I'd seen that look in Thomas's eyes before, sensed the deep-seated loneliness.

My pulse raced as I tried to catch my breath, the depiction too close to my experiences these past two weeks and the painting hanging in the study.

Why are you panicking, Madelyn?

I tried to quell the crazy theories seizing my brain. My eyes darted across the painting, searching for an explanation, and then I noticed a crack in the paint, and my frantic breath caught in my chest.

I took a tentative step closer, my grip now strangling my notebook. I squinted at the rich tones of the breeches and gasped. This painting was old, and not twenty or even thirty years old, but at least one hundred judging by the condition of the paint on the canvas. I blinked and swallowed before shifting my eyes to the signature in the lower right-hand corner. The looping letters belonged to the same artist who had painted *Der Alp*, and the signature taunted me from the painting like a warning for a disaster I couldn't avoid. I took a step back and reached out to the bed post for stability, my knees shaking as badly as the hand gripping my notebook.

And through the panic of my racing mind, the now familiar chill—that feeling I was being watched—traveled down my spine. Dread captured my emotions and adrenaline surged. I didn't want to turn around because I knew what I'd find when I did. I closed my eyes, took a deep breath, and turned to face the door.

Thomas stood at the threshold leaning against the door jamb, hands shoved into his pockets, one ankle crossed over the other. His eyes darted past mine to the painting, and then he looked down at his feet, uncertainty coloring his expression.

"Do you like what you see?" he asked, his voice low and apprehensive.

I blinked hard, not sure how to respond. I didn't understand what was happening, my mind refusing to admit what I knew in my heart had to be true.

When I didn't say anything, he pushed himself off the door jamb and took a step into the room, staring once again over my shoulder at the painting behind me.

"I had it commissioned shortly after *Der Alp*. I have always preferred this depiction of our kind to the tripe my mother had painted in the study."

He stopped a few feet away and looked at me, waiting for me to respond, but I stood frozen, unable to speak.

"I had hoped to explain everything in our own time, but..." He held his arms out and then dropped them to his sides. "Here we are," he said with a resigned, half-smile.

I swallowed and somehow managed to find words. "You're not forty-nine, are you?"

PANIC GRIPPED MY insides. She shouldn't be here. She wasn't supposed to find out this way. How would she trust me now?

I looked past her to the painting commissioned almost one-hundred and fifty years ago, my silent protest against my mother's despicable ways. Hopefully, the depiction would help her understand.

"You're not forty-nine, are you?" she asked, her quavering voice no more than a whisper.

I met her eyes and half smiled, trying in vain to affect a light tone. "Give or take a hundred and twenty years."

Her eyes grew wide.

"I stopped aging at forty-nine, so, it is a certain sort of truth."

She narrowed her eyes. "What..." Her throat worked through a hard swallow. "What are you?"

"I think you already know the answer to that, Madelyn."

"I don't believe you," she said, vigorously shaking her head. "Those things aren't real."

"I assure you. I am very real."

She looked away, struggling to come to grips with the monster standing before her. She paled as realization congealed, and she pieced together the truth, my truth. Her face transformed from an expression of shock into one of horror, and it ripped the remains of my heart from my chest. This is where I'd lose her.

"Your mother..."

"My mother was a monster. Do not confuse her black heart with mine or my father's. We left for a reason."

"The sculptures—"

"Are sculptures," I cut her off, holding up a hand. "They aren't the gravestones of fallen lovers if that's what you're thinking.

"I am not going to lie to you, Madelyn. My mother preyed on humans. She lured them here with her power. She fed on them without conscience, without care for their well-being, or how she hurt them or my father. She was sick—the worst example of my kind—and after a time we couldn't stand to watch it anymore. It is why we left."

"Did they die? Did she kill them?" Her voice had turned high-pitched and distraught.

"Not in the way you're thinking. She enthralled them, turning their desire into addiction. Once enthralled, they always came back, their need transformed into a physical reaction, their emotions and bodies attached to her even as she drained the life from them."

"I don't understand any of this," she cried, hugging her notebook to her chest as she spun away from me.

"I am not like her, not like those of my kind who only see humans as food. I keep *Der Alp* hanging in the study for that very reason. It is there to remind me of the monster my mother was, the monster I refuse to become.

"Everyone chooses what type of person they want to be. I chose long ago not to let my hunger rule my life. I would never hurt someone just to gratify my desire to feed."

"This isn't happening," she said more to herself than me and turned to eye the door behind me, looking for an escape. Then she met my gaze with pleading eyes. "I don't believe you." Her voice shook.

I took a step forward, longing to comfort her and explain.

"Believe me. As much as it pains me to admit, I am what I am. But I am also the man you have grown to know these past two weeks, the man who is falling for you. I have waited for someone like you for so long. I hoped you might accept me for who and what I am. You weren't supposed to find out this way."

I couldn't keep the desperation from my voice. I couldn't lose her and be alone again.

I STARED AT him—the incubus—standing like a stone wall between me and my escape. Nausea rose as what I believed impossible was replaced by the cold, hard truth of Thomas's true nature. The feelings of being watched and the chills down my spine right before he'd appear. The overwhelming desire any time he drew close. The power behind just one of his kisses. The glow I thought I'd imagined in his eyes...

Had he only wanted to feed from me? Was I just a source of sexual nourishment? And why did my heart feel like it was breaking?

My pulse thundered in my ears. I needed to get out of there. I needed to get away from this... this creature.

"This is crazy. Please let me go."

Thomas winced as if I'd slapped him across the face. "I am not keeping you here." His strained voice cracked with emotion. "But please. Let me explain over our dinner tonight."

I shook my head, incredulous. How could he think I'd go to dinner with him now? Did he think I'd accept this after a meal? Continue our relationship as if this was normal? Bring him into my bed?

"Oh god..."

...stealing into the homes of unsuspecting women while they slept, haunting their victims' dreams with sexual encounters...

A wave of dizziness crashed over me as Thomas's words and the memory of my dream hit me. I swallowed back a fresh wave of nausea.

"That wasn't a dream, was it?"

He didn't answer. He didn't need to. His expression said everything.

My face heated with embarrassment and fear. He'd fed on me through my dream, and I hadn't just enjoyed it, I'd begged him for it. Suddenly, I didn't know which was worse—the fact that Thomas was an incubus or that he'd lied to me about the most powerful sexual encounter of my life. My initial shock quickly morphed into a heated outrage.

"Why didn't you tell me it was real?" I shouted, my breath now coming hard and fast as I tried to rein in my conflicting emotions. "You knew how much I wanted you!"

He stared at me, eyes full of regret. "Madelyn, I—"

"You know what? Don't answer that. I'm done." I held up a hand as I cut him off, not ready to hear his excuses. I just wanted to get out of there. I took quick strides toward the door, trying to keep a wide berth around him.

He reached out and grabbed my arm. "Madelyn. Please. Let me explain."

I flinched at the contact and yanked my arm out of his grip.

"Don't! Just... don't."

I met his eyes as I spun away, and the look of pain that crossed his face at my reaction tugged at my heart in spite of myself. But I hurried past him anyway, running down the hall and stairs, and brushed past Fritz in the foyer.

"Madam!"

I ignored him, tears streaming down my face as I grabbed my coat and bag out of the closet and burst through the front door. I doubled over for a moment, trying to catch my panicked breath as horror, anger, and overwhelming sadness fought for my attention, the outcome of this entire affair far worse than the mere disappointment I'd wanted to avoid at the outset.

Then I ran to my car, threw my things in the back seat, and sped away from the mansion and Thomas von Dreiss.

I WENT THROUGH the motions of my life like a zombie for the next two weeks, back to my routine, which no longer satisfied me the way it had before. I'd tasted something different, something compelling and fulfilling on a level I hadn't known in years. My excitement for art and zest for life had been rekindled, only to be taken away again. Disappointment and sadness overshadowed my days, unfortunate since at least before I'd met Thomas, I'd been content in my complacency. Now?

Thomas's face and scent manifested in my thoughts. His expression when I ran past him haunted my dreams. What did he expect? I lived a simple, ordinary life. It was one thing to get involved with a millionaire, but an incubus? An actual mythological creature? Bizarre and unbelievable didn't scratch the surface. This situation far exceeded my threshold for the extraordinary.

He'd also lied to me, letting me believe that our dream encounter had been just that—a dream. Regardless of *what* he was, he'd broken my trust, and that stung. Why couldn't he have just come to me in person that night? No doubt he thought he had a good reason. But he'd known how willing I was, dream or not, and how badly I wanted him. Why the deception?

In all honesty, despite what he'd done, I still wanted him. Thomas intrigued me—intellectually, emotionally, physically. I missed him, couldn't stop thinking about him even though I knew I needed to. My stomach revolted at what he'd told me of his evil mother—her ruthless feeding, how she'd destroyed lives. What assurances did I have that he wasn't the same? Except I knew he wasn't. I knew it deep in my bones.

I pushed her and him out of my mind, only to have Thomas creep back into the forefront of my focus moments later. I couldn't concentrate. With mere hours left until the weekend, Friday morning dragged on. I'd already finished my work for the day and had zero motivation to start another project. Heartbroken and distracted by thoughts of what might have been, I gave into my preoccupation and searched the internet for the legendary incubi.

Hours passed as I followed links and read blurbs, much of the content repetitive and shallow. One, two sentence descriptions of old legends from different cultures of antiquity, brief mentions of regional variations, how criminals used myths to exonerate themselves of rape and abuse.

Frustration in the lack of any substantial information brought my mood even lower until I came across an encyclopedia of mythical creatures written in the early 1800s. The excerpts online contained vivid descriptions of a variety of beings from fairy tales and folklore, far more detail than any Wikipedia article or blog post, suggesting it might hold valuable information. Some enterprising person had scanned the aged pages of the unknown tome and was selling the digitized copy for fifteen dollars. I clicked and downloaded the file. Why not?

Much of the initial description echoed what I already knew. The incubi were demons, nearly indistinguishable from humans aside from their notorious good looks—understatement—and eyes that glowed when their power surfaced. Immortal beings, they needed to feed on sexual desire and pleasure to survive. The incubi hunted their prey both in their physical form and through dreams, calling to humans by creating intense, desirous need until their victims willingly gave of themselves and even enjoyed the process of feeding the incubi with their pleasure. The incubi couldn't last much more than a month without feeding, and their powers and bodies diminished quickly without sexual nourishment.

But what I hadn't expected, and what gave me pause, was an excerpt more judgement than legend. I feverishly read the text, captivated by the new information.

Long misunderstood, and unlike other demons, incubi are not inherently evil. Their charm, desirability, and ability to provide their partners with pleasure provide ample opportunity for them to feed. As long as the incubus does not continue to feed on the same partner, the impact to a human's well-being is negligible, amounting to physical exhaustion and an intense desire to couple with the incubus again, neither of which persists if they refrain.

However, the damage wrought by repeat encounters with an incubus without bonding cannot be denied. The desire of a human under an incubi's spell manifests physically, causing the victim to experience severe hot and cold spells, headaches, pain in their joints, and a burning sensation in their chest and sex organs, becoming increasingly unbearable until they are satisfied by the incubus again. The body atrophies as more and more of the

103

victim's life force is consumed through sexual encounters. Being an incubus's thrall ultimately leads to either madness or death.

But most incubi create lifelong bonds with their mates, a symbiotic relationship in which that singular connection supplies all the sexual sustenance both parties need to survive, provided they continue to feed from one another. If separated from their bond mate, any nourishment taken from other partners will only sustain an incubus for so long before their bodies wither and die.

I sat back in my chair and looked out the window next to my desk. Between the tall buildings of downtown Milwaukee, I could just make out the lakefront and the waves pounding the shore as the early December wind whipped off the lake.

Had Thomas been telling the truth about his nature, that he was nothing like his wretched mother? He'd hinted as much the night I fled. He kept *Der Alp* hanging in his study as a reminder of an incubus's monstrous potential. He'd commissioned his own painting to convey a different image of his kind. And the look on his face when I'd rushed past him in fear and disgust hadn't been contrived. I touched my lips remembering how tender he'd been when he'd kissed me.

Based on the excerpt, Thomas and I would have to bond for me to survive a relationship with him. Casual sex and incubi didn't mix. Is that why he lied to me about the dream? Had that been some misguided attempt to protect me? As a human, if I wanted more than a one-night stand, I'd have to be all in, and he'd known that. I swallowed hard at the thought.

I wasn't a risk taker; I played life safe. Taking a chance with a millionaire, baron demon fell way outside the bounds of Madelyn Frye's safe, average existence.

I stared out the window for a time, trying to tease apart my conflicting emotions. I glanced at the clock. Three. I needed distraction. I sighed and started on the consignment of an antique dining set not due for a couple weeks, hoping the work would get me through the next two hours.

A flash of color past my desk caught my eye, and I craned my neck to see around my monitor. A huge arrangement of bright red roses was coming toward me. I looked around and the only other coworker in the office looked back at me and shrugged.

The delivery man stopped at my desk. "Madelyn Frye?"

"Yes," I answered, weakly.

He placed the flowers on my desk, got out an iPad, and shoved it in front of me. "Sign here."

I scribbled something akin to a signature on the tablet, and the guy walked away as I stared slack-jawed into two dozen red roses in a crystal vase. My stomach flipped with anticipation as I searched for a card among the fragrant blooms.

My hand shook as I pulled the card from the arrangement, my name artfully written in Thomas's slashing script across the envelope.

I sank into my chair and opened the plain white cardstock.

> *My dearest Madelyn,*
>   *My days are empty without you.*
>   *I know this is difficult to understand, but I am begging you for a chance to explain.*
>   *Please know I could never hurt you.*
>   *I will wait as long as you need.*
> *Yours,*
>   *Thomas*

My throat burned with an effort not to cry, but I lost the battle. Tears overflowed my eyes and streaked down my face. I turned off my computer, not caring I still had an hour left at work. I put on my coat, hefted the weighty vase, and walked to my car while choking back sobs.

I wiped away tears as they fell on my drive back to the west side, telling myself nothing good could come of this. It would be best to let Thomas go.

My phone rang. I glanced down. Christine.

"Hey." My voice sounded strangled even through the one word.

"Well, don't we sound like a bundle of joy."

I sniffed in reply.

"Still pining over your millionaire?"

"I'm not pining."

"You're totally pining."

"Whatever."

I hadn't told Christine what really happened. How could I? It's not like she'd believe me. She'd probably have me committed. Instead, I told her a less extraordinary version of the truth—that Thomas had offered me a job, then kissed me, passionately, and asked me out. I told her he'd come on too strong and was moving too fast, so I declined, and we'd parted ways.

"Well, buck up, little camper. This too shall pass."

"I see we've devolved into movie quotes and clichés?"

"Hey, whatever works. Why don't you come over for dinner? The kid passed his driver's test and wants to show off his skills."

"I can't believe he can drive on his own." I sighed. "I think I'll pass. I doubt I'd be very good company right now anyway. I just want to be alone."

"You're moping."

"Lay off, all right?" I snapped. "I'm not pining. I'm not moping. I just… I just need…"

Silence dropped over the line as I struggled not to start crying again.

My sister cleared her throat.

"You're not going to like what I'm about to say, Mad."

"Seriously, Christine, don't. I am *not* in the mood right now."

"I have never held my tongue before, and I'm sure as shit not going to hold it now. So, listen up.

"You've done this your entire life. You take the path of least resistance, never rock the boat. And yeah, it's worked out for you. For the most part. But no matter how much you try and convince me otherwise, I know you're lonely. You're just too scared of taking a chance because you think it might upset your safe little world.

"So, he's moving fast. So, what? From everything you've told me, it makes sense—the man is genuinely interested in you. And I can tell you're head over heels for him. So, what the actual fuck, Mad? Why the excuses? For once in your life, take a chance!"

Silence descended on the line as I processed Christine's verbal slap in the face.

"Why don't you tell me how you really feel?" I mumbled as fresh tears welled.

She snorted, and I took a deep breath.

"God. Sometimes you can be such a bitch."

"I know. It's a gift."

I chuckled and let out a long, shuddering sigh. "You're right about one thing, though. I'm scared."

"I know you are," she said, her tone now compassionate and understanding. "But that's life, and if you want something to happen, you're going to have to put yourself out there. Life's too short, Mad. Take a chance for once. Please."

My sister had never said *please* to me for anything our entire lives, and here she was, pleading with me to break out of my comfort zone, something I'd always refused in the past, and she'd respected in her own way. But now? Desperation threaded her voice. In all honesty, I was desperate for me to take a chance too.

"I'm home now." I sniffled. "Thanks, Chris."

"I got you, sis."

"Love you."

"Love you, too."

I wiped my eyes again as I pulled into my parking space and braced myself to face another night alone on my couch.

I SAT AT my desk on Monday, once again preoccupied with Thomas. The flowers had been a constant reminder over the weekend of what I'd run away from. The things I'd read in the encyclopedia and my sister's tough love had left their own marks.

Daydreams filled my waking hours… him and I curled up together on my couch laughing at the television while sharing a bottle of wine; me leaning against the grand piano in his study, captivated by the music flowing through his fingers; lying in bed, entwined in each other's arms, blissfully spent from our lovemaking, yet talking deep into the night about art, history, and our future.

By Sunday night, I'd decided to hear him out, to take a chance at that future by letting him explain. My life was missing something, and for the couple weeks I'd spent with Thomas, a fresh fulfillment and joy replaced my normal complacency and bland contentment. I wanted to experience that again. But

I was still scared of taking the risk, of putting myself out there and upsetting my world. It would take time before I mustered up the courage to reach out and connect with him.

So, I threw myself into work, determined to ignore my problems for the time being. And I had a modicum of success too, proving once again that time and distance heal all wounds. Until, of course, life unceremoniously rips off the bandage and forces you to stare at the wound. My desk phone rang, and I picked it up.

"Madelyn Frye speaking."

"Madelyn. John Parker."

"Hello, Mr. Parker. What can I do for you?"

"Listen. I received an invitation this morning from Thomas von Dreiss—that client who hired us to catalog and appraise his private collection?"

My stomach clenched. "Yes, I remember."

"There's a gala exhibition of the art in his mansion. The refurbishment is complete, and he's hosting a house-warming party to celebrate. My guess? He's looking to make connections here in Milwaukee and Chicago by putting the collection on display.

"I don't need to tell you how important this event is to the firm, and von Dreiss specifically asked for you to attend. He said he wanted to recognize the brains behind the exhibition."

"I don't know what to say, sir," I replied, a combination of anticipation and dread paralyzing my brain.

"Nothing to say. You did good work for me, Ms. Frye, and you should be acknowledged. I expect you to attend this coming Saturday. I'll have my assistant send over the details."

I hesitated. "Of course, Mr. Parker."

"Excellent. See you then."

He hung up. I don't know how long I sat there, stunned, the receiver still held to my ear, but I jumped when the busy signal reverberated through my skull, reminding me to place it back on its base.

I should come up with an excuse. There were any number of reasons I could use to get out of attending the gala. Stomach flu, a death in the family, a vacation I'd planned and forgotten to mention…

But even as the excuses flew through my mind, I knew the invitation was fate pushing me forward, urging me to talk to Thomas. Life had laid an opportunity at my feet, an opportunity to take a chance, and I decided to take it. I smiled at the warm feelings filling my heart at the prospect.

A STEADY SNOW fell in the early December evening as the town car pulled into the circular drive. I stared through the back seat window watching the flakes glint in the lamplight while I waited for the driver to open the door. Mr. Parker had sent a car for me at eight, but I'd been so nervous getting ready, wanting everything perfect for my reunion with Thomas, it was already nine.

I stepped into the cold air and walked to the doorstep in awe of the transformed mansion made magical by the falling snow. I reached for the bell pull out of habit, but before I could ring it, the door swung open, and Fritz's familiar face stared back at me.

"Ms. Frye. What a pleasure to see you," he said with a smile that warmed his usually stoic features. He hurried me in out of the cold. "Baron von Dreiss will be most pleased to see you."

"Thank you, Fritz. It's good to see you, too."

He took my coat, and as he hung it in the closet, I took in the transformed foyer alive with the energy of milling guests and light from the chandelier that had sparkled to life. An elaborate flower arrangement of winterberry pansies, camellias, and hot house white roses filled the space atop the entry table, the colors artfully reflecting the crystal glow of the chandelier and the snow outside. The still-life oils we'd chosen to remain had been augmented by new pieces—ostensibly from Thomas's private collection—and the selection complemented the aesthetic. The grand entrance had turned out just as I'd imagined.

On his way back to the door, Fritz leaned toward me and whispered, "You look lovely, madam," then returned his countenance to its austere expression and resumed his station.

I smiled. Fritz had always been kind, but I'd be lying if I didn't admit to having put extra effort into my appearance. Christine had come over to help me curl and pin up my hair, and I'd bought a new evening gown for the occasion. The beaded bodice of the snug silver gown hugged my curves as if the designer custom cut the dress for me. I couldn't pass it up. I'd decided to take this chance, and I'd be damned if I wasn't going to do it right.

"Ms. Frye. Where have you been?"

My attention snapped to the voice, which came from Mr. Parker, who rushed into the foyer, his bald pate reflecting the light of the chandelier, his beady eyes alive with worry. A large man in both stature and girth, he reached out to shake my hand and squeezed it firmly as he loomed over me, searching my face for a problem.

I gave him a reassuring smile. "I'm sorry, Mr. Parker. I was running late and then it took the driver longer than expected in the snow. I'm fine."

"Thank God. I was worried sick. Well, these things happen—especially in winter. Let's get moving. Mr. von Dreiss is waiting, and I want to introduce you to a couple potential clients up from Chicago." His face lit up at the prospect. "The mansion looks top notch, no doubt thanks to your keen eye. We need to capitalize on this, Ms. Frye. Capitalize!" He clasped me on the shoulder with his massive paw, and I almost tipped over in my heels.

"Of course, Mr. Parker."

"Good," he replied, squeezing my shoulder one last time and then led me to the stairs.

As we made our way to the ballroom, we paused at each room to look inside. Guests gathered in and out of the rooms, appreciating the art as they sipped cocktails and commented on both the compositions and individual pieces. The themes we'd identified for each room came through in the selections and surrounding décor, the old pieces that hadn't fit replaced with tasteful works that enhanced our overall design. Our vision for the mansion, the vision

Thomas and I created together, had come to life, and my heart swelled with pride.

My satisfaction morphed into joy when we entered the ballroom. A string quartet played Händel in the corner between the fireplace and the French doors that opened onto the balcony. A roaring fire warmed the large space, and the glass doors revealed the falling snow, glinting in the light emanating from the room. White-clad servers balanced champagne flutes on trays as they moved between small groups of men in tuxedos and coiffed women in evening gowns no less ornate than my own. The ballroom looked like a scene transported out of the late 1800s merged with the present—the lighting, furniture accents, music, and artwork all combined with the energy of the guests to give a refined yet exuberant life to the space. The faces of the guests reflected their awe at the atmosphere we'd created, and my heart soared at getting to see the ballroom achieve its full potential.

We made our way through the ballroom, stopping so Mr. Parker could introduce me to potential clients as we went. Not once did he hesitate to announce my role in the transformation of the von Dreiss mansion.

We chatted with my former coworkers from the art museum, spoke with notables from the

Milwaukee and Chicago art worlds, and everyone we talked to complimented us on the collection and its presentation.

I tried not to seem preoccupied, which became increasingly difficult as time passed and I had yet to see Thomas. Anticipation gripped my insides like a vice, and after another half hour, I gave in, took a glass of champagne, and drank deeply to ease my nerves.

Mr. Parker was talking to the head reporter from the Arts and Culture section of the *Milwaukee Journal* when a chill crept along my spine. The familiar sensation flooded my awareness. Goosebumps spread over my arms, and my stomach flipped. Knowing the source of the chill, I bit the inside of my cheek to prevent myself from smiling like a lovesick fool. I blinked slowly, steeling my resolve, and looked over my shoulder.

Our eyes met across the crowded room like magnets pulled together by the force of their nature. For the briefest moment, his green eyes glowed with the heat of our connection. I gasped, my desire for him swelling even though a seed of fear and doubt battled my relief and comfort at seeing him again. My breath quickened as he began a slow prowl toward our location, never taking his eyes off me. His tailored tuxedo moved with the lines of his lithe body and each graceful stride, and his wavy hair fell across his forehead with boyish charm. I had to break eye contact before I blushed, so I turned back to face my boss and the reporter, my insides flush with the heat of my reaction to Thomas.

The energy—the chill—grew in intensity as he neared. And then his hand pressed against the small of my back.

"Mr. Parker. Ms. Frye. Thank you for coming tonight."

His hand fell away, replaced by a cold emptiness no less palpable.

"Mr. von Dreiss," Mr. Parker said. "Thank you for having us. We're honored to attend and that you chose our firm to lend a hand in curating this magnificent collection."

"You are too modest, Mr. Parker. I have no shame admitting that the curation of the collection you see tonight is largely due to this woman right here." He looked at me when he finished, capturing my eyes with his and speaking as if he meant the words for my ears alone. "She is a remarkable talent. One of the best art historians I have ever worked with. I was lucky to have her on this project." He held the gaze a moment longer, and my heart melted. Then he turned back to Mr. Parker. "You have a valuable asset in Madelyn Frye, Mr. Parker. Make no mistake."

MY HUNGER SURGED at the sight of her; I had to fight to keep myself in check. I had started to lose hope she would come, forcing myself to accept the inevitable, that loneliness would once again pervade my life. But then she stood in front of me, a vision in silver finery, her face turned slightly to hide her blush. She had curled and pulled up her hair, and loose tendrils brushed against the milky skin of her neck. I wanted to run my tongue along her skin until I made her cry out for more.

Her dress accentuated the delicious shape of her body, and I imagined myself buried deep inside her as I gripped those full hips and took her mouth with my own. I needed to sate the growing hunger inside me. I hadn't fed since the night I visited her; the thought of satiating my hunger with anyone but her made me sick, the need to bond with her overwhelming even my basest need to feed. I was ravenous for Madelyn, and her alone.

I didn't want to leave her side, but my guests demanded attention, and I needed distance before my hunger became stronger than my will. When Mr.

Parker engaged the reporter, I leaned into Madelyn and whispered, "Wait for me." Then I took her hand and kissed it while looking into her eyes with as much promise as I could put into my parting words.

She let out a subtle gasp before I walked away.

The night wore on, and I played host and socialite, all the while keenly aware of Madelyn's presence. My hunger grew, and my control hung by a thread knowing I might not have another chance with her.

Guests started to leave, and I watched Mr. Parker and Madelyn exit the ballroom. My stomach clenched with worry she might not heed my request and wait. Then she bid her boss goodbye and stood at the top of the stairs looking down into the foyer, and I exhaled with relief.

I found Fritz and told him to see the rest of the guests out and to not disturb us. She was wandering down the hall studying some of the new pieces I had selected when I approached. She glanced over her shoulder and froze.

I turned to make sure no one else occupied the hallway, then placed my hand on the small of her back. "Where are you going, Madelyn?" I asked as I guided her farther down the hall toward my bedroom.

She hesitated, pushing back against my hand, but I pressed her forward. She looked up at me, eyes wide, and swallowed. I leaned down and brushed the ridge of her ear with my lips. "Do you trust me?" I asked.

She stared at me with a look of wonder, as if surprised by the answer, and said, "Yes."

We slipped into my room, and I shut the door behind me. She stepped farther into the space, twisting her hands, before turning to face me. She blushed and looked away, tucking a piece of hair behind her ear.

"You came," I said, my voice strangled as I tried to control my hunger and apprehension.

"Yes. I..." She paused, looked down at her hands and then met my gaze with determination. "I wanted to see you."

I closed my eyes and swallowed, my hands flexing as I tried to control the impulse to reach out and touch her. I took a step forward. She stiffened, so I stopped.

"You will give me a chance, then? To explain?"

"I shouldn't, after you lied to me. But yes, I'm giving you a chance."

I winced at her remonstration, knowing I deserved it, and dropped my head with a nod. I searched my thoughts for the right words, the

121

explanation that would make this right. I looked back up and met Madelyn's eager eyes.

"When you have lived as long as I have, life becomes a series of repetitive scenes, each iteration lonelier and duller than the last. Friends fade in and out of your life, every loss taking with them a piece of you. Things that used to amuse you lose luster, become grey, because you have no one left to share them with, and you have been there and done that for a long, long time.

"I vowed I would never be like my mother, allow my hunger to fill that void and turn me into a monster. I only feed to survive, and when I have fed for pleasure, I have never enthralled my partner.

"I never bonded—the lifelong connection my kind is capable of making—because I never found anyone I connected with enough to risk revealing myself or endure the outcome of a failed pairing. I couldn't bear watching what it did to my father.

"And then I met you." I took a step closer, and she didn't shy away. "That first night, when you walked into my study, the color turned back on in my life. Your spirit is vibrant, Madelyn, and it resonates with my own. Your energy, your independence, your knowledge of art. Your beauty. My tortured soul is flying high for the first time in over a hundred years. You gave me hope that my solitary perdition might finally come to an end."

I stepped forward once more, bringing myself close enough to touch her, and when she still didn't shy away, I dropped to my knees in front of her, overcome with emotion as I laid myself bare.

"That night I visited you in your dreams... I was beside myself with need and fear, scared that if I came to you as a man, you would want more than I could give as an incubus. I didn't want to hurt you. I should have never deceived you. All I can do is beg your forgiveness and promise it will never happen again."

Her eyes remained fixed on mine, and in them empathy replaced trepidation. "You shouldn't have done that," she said softly with a nervous, half smile as she feigned a punch to my left shoulder. I caught her wrist and placed a kiss on the delicate skin there. She sucked in a breath. "But I forgive you, Thomas. I believe you. I trust you."

My broken heart soared, and I rose to my feet with it. Her breath hitched when I reached out and cupped the side of her face, brushing her cheek with my thumb.

"I want you, Madelyn, and I know you want me. I can feel the desire building inside you. I can taste it. Your emotions are like a drug to me, tempting me, telling me you are ready to nourish me. I want to bring you to levels of ecstasy you never thought possible and feed on your pleasure as I stare into your beautiful face. Let me give you a taste."

The air sizzled between us as I sent a surge of desire through her. She gasped, and her face flushed with heat.

"And soon, if we bond, you will experience the power of my pleasure nourishing you as well."

She trembled with need but fear still lingered in those honest eyes.

"I'm scared," she said in a breathy whisper.

"I could never hurt you, Madelyn. My life is incomplete without you. I want to cherish you for all eternity."

I had bared my soul, told her the truth, and given her what was left of my heart. My body tensed with anticipation as I waited for her to decide my fate.

THOMAS'S DEEP VOICE reverberated through me, and fear of the unknown reasserted itself, battling the raging desire that gripped my body. The presence of this sexual being standing so close to me, telling me he wanted me for all eternity, rattled my nerves.

He was an incubus, a literal demon who fed on desire and sexual pleasure, a predator. But Thomas's need ran deeper. The missing piece of Thomas's life was the same piece missing from my own—someone to share it with. He wanted a partner who enjoyed art, history, and music, a companion for his immortal journey, someone he could trust to accept him, and treasure him, for who and what he was. The man standing before me wasn't a monster, and despite everything that had happened in this house, I trusted that and accepted him.

My face flushed with heat, and my heart pounded in my chest as he ran his thumb along my cheek. His heavy-lidded eyes clouded with worry even as his jaw twitched with barely contained hunger.

Before Thomas, nothing had tempted me to live an adventurous existence. I'd always been content to move through life knowing exactly what the future held and what each day would bring. Thomas not only tempted me but compelled me toward the unknown, and for the first time in my life, the fear of taking a chance couldn't hold me back. I was ready to step out of my comfortable existence and dive into a new world just to be with this man. I wanted Thomas. I wanted his companionship, his mind, his passion.

And I knew he wanted me. He had a painful, aching need that went beyond lust and hunger, an unsatisfied emptiness he believed I could fill. In that we were the same. Weeks without him had put an exclamation point on the hole in my life. I stood on the precipice of a future with Thomas, and I was determined to take the plunge.

I leaned into his touch, my decision to embark on this new and unprecedented part of my life propelling me forward.

I stared into his sea-glass eyes and the vulnerability and hope that lived behind their haunting beauty. I knew this man's soul even after only a short time, and it was beautiful, gentle, and desperate for love. I reached up to brush the wave of hair from his forehead that always seemed to fall out of place. He closed his eyes and sucked in a shuddering breath. I lifted my other arm and entwined my fingers behind his neck.

"I want you too, Thomas," I whispered.

His eyes blazed with that intense glow I now knew signified his arousal, and his mouth descended on mine in a scorching kiss. He put his arms around my waist and pulled me to him, ravishing my mouth and my soul with a kiss that held all his desperation and promise for the future.

I surrendered, completely and with a wild abandon I didn't think possible, and the heat in my body surged with the pleasure of doing so.

He broke the kiss, gasping for air, the intensity of our connection overwhelming both of us. He leaned his forehead against mine and slowed his breath. Then he lifted a shaking hand, brushed the loose hair from my neck, and leaned forward.

Gooseflesh pebbled my skin as warm breath and soft lips caressed my neck. His hand landed on my waist, and his other slid down the nape of my neck to the zipper at the top of my dress. He pressed gentle kisses just below my ear while he pulled the zipper down past my hips. His fingertips trailed the length of my spine as he brought his hand back up to one of the silky shoulder straps. His kisses traveled to my cheek and then the corner of my mouth. My lips parted, eager to taste his tongue as he pushed the strap off my shoulder. It fell, and he transferred his attention to my collarbone as his hand moved from my waist to the other strap. With the same languid motion, he pushed the strap off my shoulder, and my dress fell to the floor.

I stood there in lace panties and heels. Thomas took half a step back and ran his fingers up and down my arms and then grazed one of my nipples with his thumb. His eyes held a faint glow.

127

"You are so beautiful," he said.

Then he picked me up as if I weighed nothing, his arm around my shoulders and under my knees. I wrapped my arms around his neck and kissed the warm skin above his collar, eliciting a shiver and rumble in his chest before he laid me down on his bed.

He stared at me as I lay there, and his gaze left me feeling sexy, sensual, and worshipped. He stepped back from the bed as he undid his cufflinks. He placed them on the end table, never breaking eye contact, and began undressing. With each slow movement of his deft fingers, with each button he undid, with each step of his erotic display, my aching need soared to new heights. He shrugged out of his crisp white shirt revealing his muscled torso.

His eyes shone brighter now, reflecting the intensity of my desire at seeing him half naked. "Touch yourself as you watch me, Madelyn," he said in a gruff, commanding voice.

I groaned at the order, my overly sensitive flesh tingling with pleasure from his words alone. I snaked my hand down past my stomach and slipped it under the lace. My fingers quested farther south until I found wetness. I dipped my finger into the warmth there and then circled my folds with my desire. His eyes brightened as pleasure spread through my body and fed him what he needed. He took off the rest of his clothes with utmost care and patience until he stood only in his boxer briefs, the muscled *V* of his abdomen and trail of dark hair leading to a hardness I knew was for me.

He walked over to the bed and climbed up, kneeling at my feet. He removed my heels, one at a time, kissing the inside of my arch, ankles, and calves as I continued to fondle myself for both our enjoyment. He reached up and pulled down the remaining scrap of lace. I lay before him exposed, my fingers wet with my desire, my raging arousal providing him a feast.

His eyes flared with hunger, and his slow, sultry motions morphed into frenetic need. He took both my wrists and pinned them over my head, pressing the bulge beneath his boxers into my heat and taking my mouth with his. He stroked my tongue mercilessly and ground himself into me. I moaned into his mouth as electric bliss shot through me from the glorious pressure of his undulating hips.

He broke the kiss, and I gasped for air as he sucked on my neck and growled, "I need more."

Adrenaline coursed in my veins at his words, but out of excitement at what came next, not fear.

He released my wrists and rose to his knees to remove his boxers. I shivered at the sight of him, so painfully beautiful as he knelt before me, his magnificent cock in his hand. He stroked himself as he reached out and massaged my breast with his other hand. The sight of this devastating man pleasuring himself as he drank in my lust was the most erotic thing I'd ever experienced, and for a moment, I thought I would climax from watching him alone.

But I wanted to feel him inside me, feel the pressure of his body. I reached up, captured his shoulders, and pulled him down on top of me. I kissed him frantically, my arms wrapped around his neck urging him closer. His warm, hard body pressed against mine, and the feel of my nipples against his chest shot a fresh jolt of pleasure through my already eager flesh.

"I need you, Thomas. Please!"

He propped himself up on his forearms and looked into my eyes, searching. Then he reached down, took himself in hand once again, and placed himself at my entrance. He brought his hand back up, cupping my face, and then he kissed me with all the longing and desire I'd seen in his eyes as he slowly pushed himself into me.

With each inch of his hard, thick length, a fresh wave of erotic pleasure danced across my body driving me closer to the edge. When he was fully sheathed, he broke the kiss, stared into my eyes, and crooked a smile. Then his eyes flared, the sea-glass green blazing with a bright iridescent light, and my body tingled with new sensations. Pinpricks of pleasure danced across my skin, centering at my core, and a searing heat sped through my veins pulsing in time with my heart. I gasped in response.

A moment of fear at the reminder of Thomas's true nature gripped my insides, but it was fleeting. My trust in him and his intentions immediately resurfaced, and fear was replaced by the excitement of being with such a sexually powerful creature.

Sensation peaked as he pulled back and started to move inside me. I moaned and came around him after only one thrust, the power of his sex shattering me into oblivion. He continued to move through my orgasm, sending shock waves through my body. Wave after wave of sexual euphoria traveled to every extremity as he continued to kiss me and grind his body against mine in slow, rhythmic motions that left me gasping.

When my body stopped shaking, he moved faster, chasing his own release, and the sensations redoubled. He lifted himself to his knees and pulled my hips off the bed toward him. His muscled body strained as he pounded his hard length into me over and over, bringing me to the edge once again. He stared down at me, his face a picture of carnal delight—glowing eyes and a wide, wicked smile. The man thrummed with sexual energy, his power expanding in the presence of our combined pleasure and desire.

And then he came. His body tensed even further, and he threw his head back as waves of ecstasy slammed into my body causing me to reach my apex yet again. I screamed out, and he groaned, our bodies shaking as he pulled my hips closer and ground himself into me, my walls spasming around his throbbing cock. He spilled into me over and over, and my body climaxed until his was complete, and he collapsed atop me.

He wrapped his arms around me as he lay panting, shivering in aftershock. He kissed my neck, and we lay like that until both our bodies calmed. Then he pulled out and rolled to his side, one leg still draped over my thighs, his fingers running along the side of my face.

"You may have just sold me on the whole bonding with an incubus thing."

His chest rumbled with laughter. Then he turned his face up to meet mine.

I looked into his eyes, no longer glowing, but no less beautiful, and filled with sincerity.

"Don't ever leave me," he whispered.

My heart clenched at the vulnerability in his voice.

I brushed the wave of hair off his forehead and pressed a gentle kiss there.

"I won't."

Six Months Later

I STOOD ON the side of the stage in the foyer of the Milwaukee Art Museum. The floor length windows looking out across the lake revealed the pristine blue waters glistening in the summer sun. I shifted my weight, my black Louboutin heels—the single most uncomfortable pair of shoes I'd ever worn—looked damn good, the perfect accent to my knee-length, cap-sleeved black dress and string of pearls. It never hurt to go with a classic.

Thomas addressed the gathered crowd of reporters and museum patrons with ease, once again looking like he'd walked off the page of a Ralph

Lauren ad in his perfectly tailored, three-piece charcoal suit. My heart clenched just looking at him. I scanned the crowd and found my parents, proud smiles on their wrinkled faces. My sister stood among the other reporters, jotting down notes and whispering to her assistant. My stomach turned over from nerves, but then I looked at Thomas, the man who had stolen my heart and given me the motivation I'd needed to take a chance, and stood a little taller.

"And so," Thomas's sultry baritone addressed the gathered crowd, "it is with great pleasure, that I introduce to you my wife, Madelyn von Dreiss, and the curator of the new, permanent von Dreiss exhibit at the Milwaukee Art Museum."

He turned to look at me, and those gorgeous eyes of his were filled with such love and adoration it nearly took my breath away. I smiled back at my husband and took a step toward him on stage. Polite applause rippled through the foyer, interrupted by a loud whoop from my sister, drawing glares from the crowd and a hearty laugh from Thomas.

Thomas held out his hand, and I took it. As I joined him at the podium, he leaned in, kissed my cheek, and whispered, "You are the most beautiful woman I have ever known. I love you, meine Liebste." He pulled away, and for a moment, his eyes glowed that mesmerizing iridescent green I'd grown to love.

"I love you, too, Thomas," I replied before facing the crowd.

As I stood before the gathered patrons, reporters, and my family, about to address the public for the first time in my capacity as the art curator for the von Dreiss family estate, I marveled at the path I'd taken to get here. Thomas and I had married after only a few short months in a private ceremony that Thomas insisted happen at his family estate in Dresden, a request I eagerly agreed to. He'd flown my entire family to Germany, and the castle was everything he said it would be. Our intimate wedding went off like a fairy tale. We spent a month exploring the estate and the art there, and I couldn't have imagined a better way to spend our honeymoon.

We'd bonded during that time, luxuriating in the prolonged sexual encounter necessary to forge the physical connection of the incubi. Thomas's desire and pleasure now nourished me as much as mine did him, and my body thrummed with the power that resulted from the bond.

We'd sealed our shared fate, tethering ourselves to one another for all eternity. The missing piece in my life, that empty seat next to me on my couch, had been filled with Thomas von Dreiss's love, and I reveled in it and him.

Behind the stage, the centerpiece of the von Dreiss exhibit, hung *Der Alp*. The piece had garnered much discussion among art critics and the museum itself, and we hoped it would create a draw for the museum. But more importantly, we'd taken the last vestige of his mother's evil out of Thomas's study and his life, removing the reminder that he was a monster, because he wasn't. I knew my husband's soul, and it was beautiful, like the painting he commissioned that still hung in our bedroom, a being who had searched far too long for partnership and love, things I promised to spend the rest of my life giving him.

THE END

Author's Note

I WAS SEVENTEEN the first time I visited the Witch's House in Fox Point, and a repurposed Snapple bottle was definitely involved. Years later, I learned that the house belonged to a lovely sculptor who created and taught art for years in the Milwaukee suburb, but the old urban legends always stood out in my mind. She died in 2001, and the house is now a Milwaukee County Landmark and preserved by an art conservancy.

Fast forward to 2022, when I became obsessed with the pulp covers of mid-century gothic romances. I spent hours browsing Pinterest, searching Google, and visiting various Twitter accounts, eager to view more examples of the compelling aesthetic. In most of the covers, a woman is fleeing from a haunted or decrepit house, the house central to the setting-as-character aspect of the gothic romance. The overwhelming sense of dread and anxiety created by the original artwork captivated me.

Inspiration hit as I connected the dots. What if the Witch's House really did have a secret? What if something untoward happened there? Could I use that house and the urban legends that surrounded it (albeit highly embellished and altered to fit my intent) to set the stage for a modern-day gothic romance? This novella is my answer to that question.

I also knew I wanted Thomas to be from Dresden, a cultural epicenter of art, music, and philosophy in nineteenth century Germany prior to its destruction by the Allies at the end of WWII. I first visited Dresden in 1995 shortly after Reunification, and it was eye-opening to see firsthand the vestiges of WWII still present on the landscape fifty years later, as if the burned-out buildings had been preserved in a time capsule. The previous year, the German government began the reconstruction of Die Frauenkirche, which had been left as charred rubble since 1945. I watched workers as they sand-blasted stone after stone, meticulously cleaning off the char so that the church could eventually be restored to its former glory. That process took until 2005.

I wanted to capture that sense of patience and rebuilding by reflecting those themes in Thomas's character. As an art collector, and an immortal, his presence in the city during its heyday and then after its destruction was an important part of the story I wanted to tell, creating a bridge through history that shows how things can be rebuilt even after such destruction and so much time. Just like Thomas rebuilds his life after a century of destruction wrought by his evil mother.

This novella is my first standalone piece of published fiction, and I'd like to thank you for taking a chance on an aspiring author by reading it. I'd also like to thank Kelly Schaub, Margaret Curelas, and especially Rhonda Parrish without whose guidance and advice I'd be completely lost. Thank you.

About the Author

KATELYN BREHM IS a second-generation German-American and native of Milwaukee, Wisconsin. She grew up watching far too much Star Trek, so much so, she decided to dedicate her education and career to space exploration. When she's not reading and writing fantasy and romance, Kat works as an aerospace engineer at NASA's Jet Propulsion Laboratory. She lives in Pasadena, California with her husband and two cats, Mini Wheat and Pepper.

Made in the USA
Middletown, DE
18 March 2023

27074181R00085